DOMESTIC RANSOM

DOMESTIC RANSOM

Vanessa Leigh Hoffman

ISBN: 0692645853
ISBN 13: 9780692645857
Library of Congress Control Number: 2016902916
VL Hoffman Productions, St. Petersburg, FL

ONE

THE KNIGHT

After attaining full consciousness, I felt riveting tingles up and down my hands and forearms, growing more massive and lengthy with every second, until they reached my shoulder blades.

My knight picked me up from the concreted fuel island and shouted to an evasive cashier, "She needs something to sit on."

No response was given by the worker.

My knight scurried around the convenience store until he found a sturdy card board box and placed me on top of it.

He caressed my hand, looking into my blue eyes all the while saying, "Don't worry. Everything will be fine. Help's on the way."

In the meantime, the hoodlum truck driver from the other side of the bay was paying inside, laughing all the while. He thought it comical that I was covered in blood from my hair down to my toes. My knight took charge. Curse words were exchanged. My knight was waiting for the hoodlum to throw the first punch, so he could legally knock him out, but the bluffing hoodlum got scared and exited the store.

The ambulance finally pulled in, after twenty painstaking minutes. Before, my knight had given his name and phone number to my best friend Kerry, so that she might be able to give him a follow-up phone call and tell him how I was doing. I smiled, my heart now beating rapidly, as if it had been hit by an arrow sent from Cupid. The vehicle quickly raced off with Kerry and me inside. I suddenly felt alone, as if I had just left a part of me behind.

Outside of the hospital emergency room, detectives were waiting to question me. It seemed the two "Dick Tracys" were trying to catch me in a grand lie, which they did not, because I was not lying. It's so easy to live life when you simply tell the truth.

My husband was waiting in the courtroom they told me, and I, the plaintiff, wasn't. No, I was laid up in what felt like an emergency room domicile for six solid hours, listening to a couple of uncaring, clever police force detectives screech on and on, giving their own versions about what happened that starlit morning.

Finally, I was dismissed, after doctors set police straight, telling them what weapons had to be used, in order to inflict wounds like these. We were driven back to the truck stop, where I gave my friend the keys to drive the thirty-foot straight job. All we had left to go was one hundred interstate miles.

The ride was going smooth, not much traffic, and great weather, until the fishtailing started. Kerry couldn't control the movement of the erratic tires. I stretched, and tried to grab the steering wheel to straighten the truck. It was too late.

I didn't see my life flashing before me, which people say is what is supposed to happen before tragedy strikes. Instead, I quickly planned my mental strategy for staying alive, not knowing what I was in store for…injury or death.

The vehicle began to wildly stray off its course. In a few seconds, the truck turned over violently and forcefully.

TWO

The Art Museum

The tornado that killed two residents in the next county earlier that day had given no warnings as to its pursuance of victims. Vicki turned off the radio and sadly drove to the art showing. Even though the sky was horridly black and the rain was gushing, she continued onward, and she didn't know why. It was not her, but a force that was driving her long, midnight blue Deville that afternoon, for some unknown reason.

Getting out of the car was a feat in itself, as her long, white-laced skirt flew up to her shoulders, and she tripped over a rock, masked by low-lying clouds. She then got a strange urgency to get the hell out of there and go home, maybe stop by John's, her friend's house.

John lived a few blocks from the mansion, which was formerly owned by Mr. and Mrs. Janssen, a very well-to-do, middle-aged southern couple who had five children. Mr. Janssen had made his fortune in the cotton trade. When Mr. and Mrs. Janssen died in a boating accident several years later, their mansion, which was located on five acres of botanical lavishness, and which displayed a grassy pavilion area in back, was profitably sold to an art association to use as their museum.

She ventured to the entrance, as this uncontrollable force suggested that she do. She entered and walked to the gift shop in back, where one of the Janssen daughters worked as a volunteer three days a weeks. Tammy was one of Vicki's closest acquaintances. Tammy looked like Vicki, spoke like her, even walked liked her. They met in college when they had the same language course.

"Long time no see," Vicki yelled across the hallway when she saw Tammy's face.

"Hey girl," was all Tammy could say, before a young, dark-haired art patron alienated her personal space and began his chase.

Next thing I knew, she was slapping his cheek, pointing to the hallway. She screamed to his back, "I would never go out with you, even if you were the last man on this god forsaken planet."

She had always been so good in class at getting her point across, Vicki thought to herself, as she shrugged her shoulders and looked at Tammy in bewilderment.

Vicki left well enough alone and began her parade down the hallways, which resembled **The Louvre** in Paris. She had always loved France, especially the countryside, where the best food in the world was made, even at cheap hotels, where she stayed frequently. These French memories swirled through her mind, until he did it. Tammy's good-looking stalker bumped into her, seemingly on purpose.

Vicki acted offended, but she was really very flattered. He had the best looking face she had ever seen, up to that point. He made her heart flutter and her mind forget everything it had ever learned in eight on and off again years of acquiring a Bachelor of Art degree.

He appeared to be a trifle heavy in his mid-section, but that was alright to her. The mystery man spoke so eloquently, "I love French impressionism. Do you?"

She said, "It's my favorite."

He just smiled, smiled as they walked, almost together, almost as a couple.

When they finished the inspecting of paintings, he walked out to the garden, through the exit. Vicki followed, silently. He pulled out a chair from one of the tables on the veranda, and a pen and paper from one of his pockets of his loose fitting khakis, which were hidden by a bulky, non-figure enhancing heavy, wool sweater. He wrote several metered poetic phrases and began to make her fall in love with him with his sweet serenity. Tammy viewed this display from a window and vowed never to speak to Vicki again.

"Wanna get a beer and cheese dip with me up the street at 'The Grill'?" he boldly asked her.

She said, "Sure, I'll meet you there."

Thinking back on that evening now, it almost sounded like a rehearsed script to Vicki.

When Vicki arrived at *The Grill*, she realized that she still didn't even know the young man's name. She excitedly ran up to the door, opened it, saw the noisy crowd inside, and the young man sitting in the middle of it, expounding on some topic.

He glanced up, saw her, and shouted to the customers, "This is the new love of my life. Could you all please be so kind as to let her have a place to sit next to me? We must get to know each other inside and out." He had all the right lines and moves.

"By the way, I'm Victoria Morris, Vicki to all my friends and acquaintances," she confidently stated, reaching out her hand to his.

"The pleasure is definitely all mine, *mi querida*. My name is Benjamin Burks, Ben to all my friends and acquaintances," he mockingly smirked.

The two talked until the outside air turned frigid and dark, barely touching the cheese dip they had ordered, but swigging down light beers. Ben pulled out the paper he had scribbled on earlier, along with his fancy ball point pen, and began to finish his dripping, sentimental poetic nonsense.

When he was done, he capped off his writing with a wet kiss on her parched lips and drew a heart with an arrow piercing straight through it onto the back of her right hand.

He demanded, "I've got to see you again, and soon. How about tomorrow afternoon at three by the lake in Autumn Park? I'll bring Italian bread, cheeses, and salami. You bring the wine."

Ben got up from the table, pushed in his chair, and kissed Victoria's hand.

"Until tomorrow, *fraulein*," he recited, as he walked to stage left, then backstage, then onto the sidewalk.

And so the pendulum swings…

THREE

THE PARK

Vickie could hardly believe how she was feeling inside. She tried not to show it to her co-workers at the travel agency, and she tried not to feel her emotions, which was fairly easy to do, as her work was mounting up daily. The agency had a promotion with a local reality company, "Creighton Realty Mortgage".

Vicki booked their top-producing agents on wonderful paid trips to Tahiti. This proved very time-consuming, due to lack of availability for spring travel weeks. Every now and then during the day, however, Ben would call.

"Hey baby, whatcha doing later on?" he asked.

"I'm hoping to meet you tonight at the park, okay?" she would always reply.

They met at the park at eight sharp, when she got off work.

Ben grabbed and squeezed Vicki whenever he saw her. They would usually end up in the vacant parking space next to her Deville, wrapped together in love and merriment. One day, however, they both noticed a patrol car driving up on the other side of the park lane. The couple quickly got back inside the car, but not fast enough. The cop car pulled up right alongside them.

"What's up guys?" the policeman asked.

"Oh, nothing, officer," Ben answered, feeling very awkward. Then he stared at the officer's face, which was being flooded with illumination from his own flashlight. He realized the officer was a former football teammate of his from high school.

"Is that you, Rob?" Ben pried.

"Is that cannon kicker Ben? What've you been up to man?" the astonished officer shouted.

"Sorry, we're just acting like teenagers," Ben muttered.

Officer Taylor stated, smiling the whole while, "I don't know what you're talking about. I didn't see or hear nothing. Now get on out of here. Give me a call at the station sometime, you hear?"

Ben smiled and put Vicki's car in reverse and drove to his car.

This went on for three months almost on a nightly basis, meeting in the park for love. Officer Taylor never questioned them again, even though they saw him regularly patrolling the park grounds. Ben never asked Victoria about her past, during their interludes, and she never about his. They loved their relationship being this way.

"Live life like it's going out of style. That's the only way to do it," he wrote in his manuscript journal one night, while in the park with Vicki.

Finally on one of these dates, Vicki asked "Are you seeing anyone else?"

Ben answered, "Why? You're all that I want, Vicki. And what about you? Are you with anyone else?"

Without a moment's hesitation, she blurted out, "Yes, well I was…I was engaged when I met you, but it's over now. It was never a real strong commitment in the first place on either party's part. I ended it."

Ben responded wild-eyed, looking at the scratched clock on his dashboard, "Well, it's a good thing! Wow, babe. It's late. I've got an early day tomorrow at Mr. Ratchett's place. I'll call you tomorrow."

She got out of his beat-up clunker and into hers, without turning his way.

Three days passed with not one phone call. On the fourth day, while eating breakfast alone at a coffee shop near her house, Ben finally called. He asked Vicki to come over to the house where he worked. Ben told her that his duties were to take care of an aging former professor of psychology who was schizophrenic, manic depressive, an artistic genius, and a homosexual, who lived with his young partner. Vicki thought this odd that this professor would employee Ben to watch over him when he had his own lover there with him, twenty-four-seven.

When she asked him why, Ben responded with, "They just posted this notice about work available as a babysitter for an adult on the wall of my psychology professor's office. I called. We arranged an interview, and I got the position. It doesn't pay great, but it pays my bills, while I'm living at grandma's, anyway, and I can spoil you with the money, too."

Vicki just stared at him with wonderment. Had she forgotten something, or had he never taken her anywhere for what seemed like a very long while. Her contemplative mood was broken by his eyes, staring through her, through the phone. She felt them.

"Let's go to *The Grill*, like we did at first. I want you to order anything on the menu. I want to treat my wife-to-be like a queen."

Vicki didn't utter a phrase, not even a sound.

"Did I shock you?" was all he asked.

FOUR

THE SETTLEMENT

Ben called Vicki on the fifth day of not seeing each other and invited her to visit him at his "work". He met her out front, then escorted her back to a shed where tools were kept. He unbuttoned her pink blouse and started sculpting her anatomy with his hands. At that moment, a muscular man of about thirty swung open the door to the tool shed, and entered.

"I guess I came to see you at the wrong time," he sarcastically remarked, and stood in front of them. Both of them were now naked. They put on their clothing and ran off to the street, got in her Cadillac, and left the scene of the crime.

As they left, a steady stream of balloons flew up to the heavens. They both thought this to be a sign from God. God and the devil tragically appear to be as one sometimes, when Satan acts benevolent.

Ben lost his job because of this encounter, which gave him more time to start writing a screen-play about supernatural forces found in graveyards. He called her at the end of each day, only to say he was too tired to see her. But he talked to her for hours, until one or two in the morning, as they watched "Friends" together.

He would read Vicki one chapter of his writing at a time, then bid her goodbye, after saying how much he loved and missed her. It seemed that he was in a perpetual trance, a trance that had locked him into this weird mental state, as she now realized.

Since they didn't speak much about their past, she never had an opportunity to tell Ben about her for-mer marriage, and how it had affected her so. The bank had called her the day prior and suggested that she put her funds from the settlement in one of their high interest mutual funds. They sent her a pamphlet on their product, which she put on the backseat of her car.

When he got into her car the next evening to check-in to the cheap hotel room he had reserved for both her and him, as he was tired of making love in the park like teenagers do, he noticed a thick folder in Vicki's backseat. He pulled it out and asked her what it was.

Vicki had wanted to keep all of her money affairs private. Now, however, she felt an obligation to tell her significant other about her divorce settlement, which was rather minimal. For a man of twenty-five, who barely had an income, and who lived in a rickety house with his grandmother and aunt, it probably seemed like a fortune she figured.

Needless to say, Victoria had to use her budgeting expertise to get her through each and every month, with a used-car payment, and a soon to be used-house payment, things were tight. Ben had no idea how valuable money was. He spent it like it would always be there, like there was no end in sight. He viewed money the same way that he viewed life, like there was no tomorrow.

"You have to take it while you've got it. It's all about TODAY, not TOMORROW!" he would tell his customers, whenever he had some.

Ben did designing and painting work on the exterior of stores and the interior of houses. In some of these fancy homes, he worked on the master bedrooms, of course only when the single mother who owned the property was home alone. He did this on a part-time basis, when he was out of *dinero*. Shortly afterward, word got around town about Ben's expertise in certain "venues". He definitely was committed from that point on to *play hard and work hardly*. He thought the rewards to be staggering!

Victoria was to sign on a house next month, in June, but until then, she lived with her socialite sister in a small house in a posh section of Memphis. Vicki placed a portion of her divorce proceeds in a mutual fund, a bit in government funds, and a bit for a new house. She thought her one hundred thousand dollars would go a long way in a little time. Later, she found out differently.

As she drove to sign the contract at the bank, Vicki informed Ben that this money was a token of what she had saved from her work proceeds. Also, there were bits she was able to contribute to her savings along the way. The check that she presented the mortgage company was for forty-five thousand dollars.

Ben asked, "Didn't you get any more than that from the bastard?"

Victoria looking shocked said, "Oh, just a little. Don't you worry about my financial affairs, okay? My ex did alright by me, and that's that. If you need more money, you go get a job and help us out, asshole."

He took the hot coffee she was sipping and spilled it all over her new, white tailored pants.

He shouted, "You slut. Stop spreading your legs while you're driving for all the truck drivers to see. Drop me off here."

She let him out. He walked into the night, or into somebody's house where he had been before.

Vicki could barely drive home she was so devastated. She had never experienced anything like this before, in all of her almost thirty-seven years of existence. She wondered what she had done to cause this and suddenly felt guilty, guilty for being pretty, guilty for wearing flattering pants and heels, and guilty for being in love with a man who was eleven years her junior. She looked younger and more vibrant than her age. He looked eloquent and chiseled. Everyone they met, wherever they went, thought they made a fabulous couple. No one knew the truth.

FIVE

ELVIS' HOT DOGS

B en was now designing a store window for a cigar shop owner whom Victoria had known through a former travel agency of which she had been a partner for a short year. The owner's name was Otis Sommersham. He had shown Victoria two passports that he possessed, one from Canada and the other from Mexico, where he was born.

He had been born on a coffee plantation in Veracruz. He lived there with his parents and sister until he turned twenty. Then, he proceeded to become a target for the FBI, the border patrol, and the U.S. Marshals. Vicki didn't know about any of his escapades with the law. All she knew about Otis was that he had been married four times, had three children, and had lived in many countries.

Well, he was now in her neck of the woods, trying to start a charter-flight service to Veracruz from Memphis. He wanted Victoria to be a part of this. He was certain that his girlfriend, Elaine, who had recently inherited one million dollars, would be the sole business start-up contributor. He stressed to Vicki that if their flight service failed, it would be Elaine's money lost, not theirs, so there was no risk at all for the two of them.

Vicki had been to Elaine's residence to deliver tickets to the couple one time in the past.

Otis made a blatant move on her, while waiting for Elaine to return home from her restaurant, *"Elvis' Hot Dogs"*, across the street from Graceland.

Vicki retrieved her belongings and exited the house, with Otis chasing behind her all the while saying, "Vicki, I didn't mean anything bad. I'm sorry. I hope this doesn't ruin our personal and business relationship."

Victoria kept on walking, got in her car, and peeled out of the gated driveway.

Otis called Vicki one month later, apologized again, and asked her if she could recommend a decorator for a new cigar shop he had just purchased. She gave him Ben's name and number, and Ben was offered the job.

Ben had been so sweet over the past month, getting back in Vicki's good graces after the stint he had pulled in her car with all his mean words. Vicki had bought tickets for them to be guests at a big blues show on Beale Street, where they later watched the stars in the sky, ate dinner, and eventually walked back to the cigar shop. That is where Otis had invited them to join him after the show.

He had three empty chairs awaiting Ben and her, and some unknown identity. This charming male identity arrived just after they did. He was a supposed high-ranking official in Mexican politics. It did not matter to Vicki at all who the man was. She was just having a nice time in the cool night air, with the sound of crickets and tree frogs all around her.

Ben was smiling and laughing. Vicki was loving it, thinking how glad she was that she had subordinated herself and apologized to him, and how lucky she was to be so much in love with this wonderful, hard-working man.

As Ben glanced her way, Ben started looking her up and down. She smiled, flattered. He looked away in disgust.

He didn't speak to her until they were alone in the car, then he laid it all on her.

"You slut, spreading your legs out so that politician could see your twat."

Vicki laughed so hard that she opened the door to get some air and fell out of her seat. She did not mean to give Ben the wrong impression. She was just feeling comfortable and having fun.

When Victoria finally regained her composure, she sternly advised Ben, "First of all, I'm not a slut, and don't ever call me that again."

And once again, they didn't speak to each other, not for the rest of the ride to Ben's grandmother's house in the hood. She grew more and more confused, more and more with each passing day. She became more and more unsure of herself, more and more with each passing day, but the strange thing was that she was still falling more and more in love with Ben, more and more with each passing day.

SIX

A MEETING OF MINDS

Vicki worked hard and long at work at the travel agency, day in and day out, leaving after six most nights. She would then go to homes to tutor Spanish, German, French and English to a variety of children, five days a week. She had no life, only Ben, if you would call that a life. So when she didn't hear from him for three days in a row, after leaving numerous messages, she sank into depression.

Vicki had always been a good student, a good daughter, just a good all-round girl. She was very pretty, with her ash-brown hair that was cut in layers. Her striking haircut and color made her medium-colored topaz eyes stand out even more.

Men always stopped to stare at her, but when she began to speak, they became disinterested.

She was too analytical, smart, and practical, and too naive and vulnerable for most men, who wanted a challenge. Vicki would give in too quickly and easily, with no struggle at all, so when Ben found her, he knew she was the perfect pawn for what he wanted in his corrupt, vicious, and *psycho* world.

Victoria was born into world of inherited money. Her parents had been hippies in the sixties. Her father went back to school, majoring in business, and eventually opened what became the leading advertising agency in the Mid-South. That coupled with her mother's family inheritance, enabled her mom, dad, sister and her to live a rather opulent life. The family traveled together around the world on several occasions.

Victoria's sister, Millicent, was only fifteen months younger than she was, looked like Vicki, but acted totally different. Millie was the party animal of their posh, private high school, getting laid every chance she could.

Millicent got her "scarlet" reputation during her sophomore year, when after the game, her drunk, winning football team took turns with her in back of the cleared-out grandstand.

She was perpetually screamed at and grounded by her parents. Mr. and Mrs. Morris eventually threw their hands up in the air and let her go her separate way. They never saw or spoke to Millicent again.

One year later, when Millie was nineteen and Vicki was twenty, both parents died in a head-on collision, as they were headed home after attending an advertising awards ceremony in downtown Memphis. The Morris money was gone, Vicki was notified by the family's attorney. She wondered how that was possible. What had happened to it?

Losing her posh house in Memphis, beautiful, tantalizing Millie ended up as an alcoholic bartender, and she bought a cheap, manufactured home in Brevard County, Florida, having no money of her own.

Millicent had never married, had always lived alone, and so Vicki had always felt the need to live near her sister. The sisters were never close as children, but became closer as they got older. Vicki constantly felt obligated to care for others in need, and right now, it happened to be her own flesh and blood.

At the end of the week, when driving back from work, her cell rang. She ecstatically answered the call.

"Ben, I'm so glad you're alright. I was so worried."

"Yeah, I'm okay," he replied. "Hey, we've got to talk. How about if I come over right now? I'm in the neighborhood." He didn't wait for a response. A dial tone invaded the line, then there was a knock on the back door. She looked out the window. It was Ben.

Answering the carport door, he barged right through, and sarcastically said, "Glad you didn't wait for me to help you move in."

"Well, I couldn't," she emphatically stated. "You wouldn't answer the phone. Why are you acting like this anyway, baby? I didn't do anything. I love you," she put a partial grin on her novice, worry-ridden face.

Ben hugged her so hard, it made her feel like she couldn't breathe. He begged her, "Please stay with me. I know I haven't been that great to you lately, but I've had a lot on my mind, you know, trying to find a job where I can support you the way I'm supposed to, the way my grandfather did with my grandmother.

I'm sorry, babe. You are definitely the farthest thing from being a slutty girlfriend. I love you, please…please…take me back."

Looking up into his melancholy eyes the entire time he pleaded, she finally broke down and started sobbing, "Yes, yes, of course I will take you back.

I'm sorry you feel kind of low. I know you want to help out more, and will eventually, and I promise to be more patient with you.

I'm doing okay. Now, I am an official language tutor. I did it all on my own, by placing an ad in the 'Neighborhood News', so we're good for a while. I want you back. Move in with me, now, tonight."

"Guess what? I was hoping and praying that you would say that, so I took the liberty and packed two bags. They're out in my car."

"Oh, and that's another thing," she said. "Tomorrow, we're going to buy you a brand new used jeep. I can't be seen in this neighborhood having a boyfriend who looks like you, driving a disgusting thing like that," she jokingly rambled on, putting her hands on the banged-up pieces of chrome.

Ben retrieved his bags, came into the den, put the bags on the floor in front of the wood-burning stove, and pulled out a large Caribbean real estate magazine. Vicki was busy preparing spaghetti with pineapples and sausage, his favorite. It had the usual heavy garlic and oregano taste, but with an extra added sweetness from ripe pineapples, and spiciness from the hot ground sausage. Ben had raved on and on about this dish which he always prepared.

One day, Vicki surprised him at her sister's and made it. Ben's concoction turned out to be exceptional when Vicki made it, and only very good when he prepared it.

Victoria was an excellent cook and always had been, ever since she was a child and had to prepare meals daily for her parents to eat when they came home from their busy work place. Her parents had an advertising agency and were busy twenty-four-seven. She didn't seem to mind, however. The family had nice houses, plenty of food, but not a lot of quality time together. Occasionally though, Vicki and her mother, or the whole family, would take a trip throughout the country, or around the world, all of the time for her parents' business.

Her mother never invited Millicent to accompany Vicki and her when the two traveled by themselves, because she knew Millie did not like to leave her "reign" at the high school. Furthermore, her mother didn't want Millie to get into any trouble, when her husband was not with them. Vicki always went gladly.

Victoria had few true friends, but she played lots of sports, and turned out to be a fairly good athlete. In general, she had a good childhood.

Ben hemmed and hawed, trying to find the right time to talk about something. He kept holding the real estate magazine and folding it up between his palms, as if nervously wringing out the pages. He was silent, simply staring at the ground, until Victoria sheepishly questioned him.

"What's wrong? What is it?"

"Nothing's wrong. Everything's right," he blurted out, in a slight stutter. "There's this great opportunity to buy a place in a gated community on the beach in Honduras. The house is only fifty thousand dollars, and you on have to put down five to reserve the lot, and you better hurry. There are only six left."

"What?" she asked him, in a state of oblivion. "What?" she asked him again.

That was all she could say. She was in a state of amazement. She went into the kitchen to pour a glass of spicy Red Zinfandel to straighten out her nerves, Ben following like a puppy dog behind her.

"Don't you see what this could mean for us, babe? We could have two places, and four incomes. When the tourist season was hot, you could go down there and work in the industry, and when it was cold, well, *you move your pretty self back up here*, and start teaching, or doing travel agency stuff at the same time. You know, like you're doing now.

As for me, I'm trying to get my construction license, then my business going, so that I can build anything, anytime, and in most places. We could really make a killing, and make a bundle on top of that when we sold it, if we ever did. It looks like a keeper to me. What do you think? Are you game and ready to become a millionaire, and fast?"

Vicki stressed, "I've got to think about this. I don't have tons of money, but I guess I could manage to scrap together a few thousand to hold the place. Give me some time."

Ben put his hands up, as in a truce, and said, "Okay by me. I'll go to Collierville for a couple of hours. If you decide to do it, I have to put a check in the mail tonight. I told him I would."

"Told who you would?" Vicki questioned him sternly.

Ben replied to her by saying, "Oh, just the realty guy in Florida. He told me that another couple wanted to send a check in tomorrow or the next day to reserve our property. Baby, he is selling us the best parcel on the property, just because of me. I told him that we would slip in an extra one hundred dollars, just to make the deal worthwhile, and he ate it up," he laughed with supreme confidence. "I'll be back soon," his voice trailing off, as he left the house.

Vicki pondered and pondered over the situation, until she came to a solution. She could teach Spanish, the subject she had majored in, during the summer, when the Americans traveled down there, and teach Spanish during the fall, winter and spring for American middle school students, of which she was accustomed. Of course, she always had to dabble in the travel business, as well.

When he arrived at the back door three hours later, close to midnight, Vicki knew he was different than when he left. She opened the door, and a strong whiff of marijuana came in behind him.

She gasped, pushing away him and the fumes coming from his nose and mouth.

Ben's eyes were red and half shut.

He was not using proper English when he said. "Hey, baby. What's the mutter? Ya wanna do it or what?" he spoke, as he stumbled off, trying to find an empty chair to sit on, as the house was still piled high with boxes from the move.

Vicki put him to bed in the guest bedroom, and trailed off to bed herself. She felt like she needed to be far away from this situation, but couldn't remove herself from it, for some reason. They both fell asleep quickly in their separate bedrooms, one because of a drug-induced state, the other because of nature and circumstance.

Vicki was now beginning to put the pieces of the puzzle of Ben's life together, as she uneasily dreamed. She had seen the horrible environment in which Ben lived and had been raised. The small house was filled with ratty furniture, dishes and pots and pans piled high in the sky. Also, mildew clung fast to every wall on the premises. She was sure that roaches had made homes for themselves inside the walls, where they slept during the day, and partied hearty at night.

Victoria had met Ben's family on a couple of occasions. His grandmother was almost an invalid, sweet, but crass. His aunt, who was younger than Vicki, was a non-working, drug-addict, who also had a young son to raise. Cat, as she called herself was a nice woman, but had no idea about work ethics, or how to survive, without being taken care of by others.

To Victoria, it was an extremely sad and bad situation, because everyone in the household seemed to always be angrily screaming at one another. They obviously did not know how to make anything work, so that they could live their lives to the fullest.

In her dream state, she realized why Ben was the way he was. He had lived with raunchy influences, in addition to an almost non-existent mother, and a never before seen dad. She muttered in her sleep, "I have to make this work. I just have to."

SEVEN

His New Toys

A sales contract was sent FedEx from Boca Raton two days later for Vicki to read over and sign. Artists' renderings of their proposed wrap-around porch bungalow were included in the packet. She read over the agreement and payment schedule over her morning coffee and Danish, signed it and included a signed check for five thousand dollars, then got the return envelope ready for mailing. She laid it on the table by the back door, so she wouldn't forget it when she left for work.

Ben had numerous job interviews that had been provided to him through temporary job brokers. He had awakened Vicki with a kiss before he left, while stroking her hair.

"Wish me luck," was all he said before he scrambled to get into his jalopy.

She thought once again of how Ben desperately needed new transportation. She thought to herself that after work, they will go to the dealership near the house and buy a jeep.

"He needs it," Vicki said out loud, as she mentally formulated a payment plan. She realized that she was now getting in a little deeper than she would like, but she was not able to rectify the situation.

"You have to spend money to make money," she kept saying to herself, all the way to work.

At the office, Vicki found out she had been a victim of a terrorist scam operation a month prior. A Middle-Eastern man named Dr. Mohammad Hussein had purchased a one-way air ticket from Chicago to Los Angeles. Vicki had taken his credit card number, which it turns out, had been falsified. She printed the e-ticket, ready for him to pick up at O'Hare.

David Callahan of the Federal Bureau of Investigations' terrorist unit in Dallas called "Leisure Days" and asked to speak to travel agent sine-in 00009. Victoria was placed on the line. She told the agent what had transpired. Mr. Callahan said that this man has been posing as a doctor from Ohio for three months now, but he was really a terrorist from Pakistan. The agent warned her and anyone at the agency not to even take a call again from any person fitting that description.

"Since you also handle a massive amount of government air traffic, it could be a very scary situation. Everyone must be careful," the agent emphasized. "Be careful of everyone you meet."

Vicki left her office in a hurry after this, panic stricken. She went to *The Grill* up the street for a drink to knock herself out after this revelation. She began to reminisce of meeting Ben in this bar, at the same "two-seater" she sat at now. Tears filled her eyes, with both happiness and sadness. She knew why she felt happy, because she was alive and excited, and pretty much secure, but she didn't really know why she also felt sad and unfulfilled. Something was just not quite right, but she didn't know what. She ordered three daiquiris, until she felt no sadness whatsoever, only happiness, and she carefully drove home.

She was met at the door by a smiling, waving Ben, whose face changed immediately, when he saw Vicki laughing, trying to fit her key chain in her wallet.

"You drunken slut! Where were you and who were you with?" he screamed, for the entire neighborhood to hear, as he started playing the victim in the relationship.

"I had something to drink at *The Grill*. I was alone. I sat at our table," she whispered, trying to pull him close to her.

He knocked her arms and hands from around his neck and said, "I'll see what's really going on around here, doll." He grabbed the keys that were in Vicki's wallet and peeled out of the sloped driveway in her Cadillac.

Vicki crouched down on the concrete floor and cried uncontrollably. She then realized, this was definitely not right. She knew she loved Ben madly and knew there was only one way left, to try to change him. She tried to convince herself that.

"It can be done. I've seen it on *Lifetime*. I just need to be strong and patient."

The next morning, Ben came home.

Vicki excitedly opened the door for him, and said, "Where have you been?"

He replied, "Oh, I've been in a horse field south of Collierville all night, clearing my head. I missed you. I'm sorry. I won't ever act that way again. I'm all messed up, you know, with my job instability. I want to give you something each month."

"Still...that's no reason to act like an imbecile," she remarked. "But it's alright. I understand."

After a few seconds of silence, she asked him, "Hey, you want to get a jeep this afternoon?"

"Sure, we'll at least look," he answered, trying to act cool.

They went to a jeep dealer one mile away and picked out a 2000 Jeep Cherokee that they couldn't resist. With forest green shine and tan interiors and a price tag of only seven thousand dollars, they couldn't resist the temptation.

Vicki wrote them a check. She followed him in her Caddy to *The Grill* where they went to celebrate. They sat at their table, where they ordered Rib-eye steaks, medium rare, and champagne, and of course, Vicki footed the bill.

She started thinking to herself, "When is he ever going to take me out again, like he used to in the beginning?"

When they arrived back home, they were greeted by an incessant beeping coming from the message machine, flashing one message.

She pushed in the play button and heard, "Congratulations, Vicki. Because of high dollar sales on our cruise line, you have been awarded with a free four-day cruise for two on the 'Big Green Boat'. You can schedule your cruise for anytime this month or next. You will be reserved a higher deck cabin with a double bed. Give us a call, soon."

Vicki picked up couch pillows and started tossing them into the air, celebrating. Ben walked into the living room to see what all the commotion was about, and she threw him a pillow. They got into a pillow fight, laughing all the while. Both out of breath, they fell on the couch, still laughing and holding each others torso.

Ben then jumped off the couch and shouted, "Let's look at my jeep once more before we turn in, okay?"

Vicki nodded.

They went out the front door.

While Ben was gazing at his rims, Vicki walked around the corner and back to the front door to look for a camera. She began to spy an older sports car slowly coming toward her on her side of the street.

The car slowed down, and the man inside pulled out his sleazy parts and started shaking them at her, saying, "You like these, don't ya, kid? Come on in for a ride with me. I promise you won't want to return, ever."

Vicki ran through the front yard and into the back trying to find Ben.

"Ben, Ben, Where are you?" she frantically yelled, searching for his handsome face, but he was nowhere. She simply waited for him outside.

Ten minutes later, he came running out of the back door of the young female next door neighbor's house.

Vicki screamed, shaking all over, "Where have you been, and why?"

Ben interjected with, "Vicki, Lori asked me if I could tighten a screw for her, and then we just ended up talking for a while. It was all innocent. Don't concoct these things. Your mind is frazzled. You've just been working too hard. You'll see, once we take the cruise. I guarantee you, everything will be superb."

She pushed him away from her and screamed, "Let me talk. You don't know what I've just gone through. This freak pulled up to me and showed me his cock. Thanks for being there for me," she sarcastically said to him.

"What did he show you? What color and make of car was it, and was he old or young, blonde or dark?"

Vicki shouted, "A red sports car, and he was older and blondish."

"I'm going to kill him," Ben yelled, as he sprinted down the street.

Vicki just threw her hands up in the air. There was nothing she could do to ever change his ways, it seemed, even though she wanted to ever so desperately. She just had to wait, like always.

"I know he's good down deep. He helps around the house, says nice things to me, mostly, wants to get a job to help me, so much so that it's making him simply crazy. Maybe he'll settle down now, since he borrowed money from me to get a jeep," she wrote in a tablet, as she drifted off to sleep in their bedroom, while watching spy flicks on cable.

Ben returned, like always, several hours later, with a sinister look on his face.

"He got away from me, but I almost had him," he praised himself. "I'm turning in. Do you mind if I join you, my dear?" Her perplexity evidently shone through her eyes.

Ben asked her, "Hey, what's the matter now?"

His all of a sudden new attitude and new personae had changed much too quickly for her to understand.

"I'm just tired," she said, and turned over.

EIGHT

The Big Green Boat

On Wednesday mornings, Vicki went in two hours later, at ten, so she treated herself to croissants and good, strong coffee, and a bubble bath. This Wednesday, however, was different. Ben got a call from the temporary job agency, and they said that a large international corporation in town wanted him to work for them as a customer service representative, as soon as possible. The pay was twelve dollars an hour, and the work was scheduled to only last for six months.

He told them he would take it and be right down to sign the papers.

"Before you go sweetie," Victoria reminded him, "don't we both have somewhere to go to...soon... together?"

"Oh yeah," he frowned, knowing he had no way out of this commitment. "Well, let's take the cruise this weekend, can we? That way, I should be back in time to start in the middle of next week," Ben sighed, knowing he was going to keep both of his supporters happy.

"I'll see what I can do," she frowned.

After she filled up the tub with water and bubbles, she stepped inside slowly. The water was only tepid. She turned only the hot water nozzle on to give her bath a hot edge. She liked it that way. It relaxed her mind, and her muscles. She slowly climbed in, and she placed her cell phone on the ledge of the tub.

After lathering and scrubbing, Vicki thought it the time to call the cruise line to find out when she could take her free cruise.

She dialed the toll-free number and got an on-hold recording of luscious island melodies, waves crashing and birds singing, next a deep-voiced woman came on the line and began to accentuate the benefits of cruising with the *Big Green Boat*.

The same music and same deep-voiced woman droned on and on in her eardrum, until a whiny-voiced, young woman, named "Pam" answered the call and apologized for the wait. Vicki introduced herself as one of the travel agents who had won a cruise for two, because of her high sales.

Pam said, "Excellent. I'm ready to book whenever you are."

Vicki asked, "Is there any way it would be possible to take this cruise on Friday?"

Pam verified, "This Friday, right?"

"Yes!" replied Vicki, almost pleading.

"That's awful soon. Let me see," and she put Vicki on hold.

She came back on the line five minutes later with good news.

"We can squeeze you guys in on this cruise for a fifty dollar expediting fee. You'll have to pick up your documents when you arrive here at the counter. Please be sure to bring two forms of government identification with you, otherwise, you will not be permitted to board. You must bring a passport, and either a driver's license, or a government-issued identification card. All I need for you to do is fax me over the two full names today, give me a credit card number to take care of the fifty dollars, and you are good to go."

Victoria heaved a sigh of relief and said, "Thank you. Thank you so much. You don't know how we need this break!"

"Oh, I know," the reservation agent coupled her emotion. "I feel that way every day. Have a great time, and again, thanks for selling *The Big Green Boat*."

At the sound of the dial tone, she realized that she would be late for work, if she didn't get a move on. She thought to herself while drying off and putting on lotion that Ben would be so pleased with her now. She really hoped he got the job, not just to help her, but to help his own self-esteem.

"He really is a great guy, no matter what he might do at times, and no matter what people might say about him. I know he loves me," she sang in a made-up monotone melody to herself in the mirror.

Friday morning's blaring alarm sounded with a start, as the two had stayed up late the night before, packing and watching video tapes of Cary Grant movies. They had fixed themselves spaghetti with crumbled Italian sausage, popcorn with mustard and cayenne pepper, and decadent hot fudge sundaes with firm whipped cream and sweet cherries on top. They were still plenty full from the night before, so Vicki didn't even bother with breakfast, just coffee. They quickly showered and dressed, then called a taxi for the airport.

The propeller plane flew to Orlando fairly smoothly, until the left side took a sudden turn to the right and spiraled downward. The passengers panicked. The pilot eventually righted the small aircraft, then flew as if nothing had happened. He didn't even make any kind of an apology or explanation as to what had occurred. Everyone fell silent, until the plane landed and the doors were opened, then they all gossiped like a bunch of cackling farm hens. She was then happy they were not able to get a ticket back at the last minute and had to book a rental car.

After the cruise bus picked them up at the terminal and drove them to the pier on the cape, the two checked in at the counter and were given a cabin assignment. It just so happened to be a mini-suite overlooking the water on the top deck.

"What classy shit!" Ben proclaimed to Vicki.

She nodded.

As he smiled slyly, he thought to himself how many women he would be able to meet on a ship like this, having an ocean-front suite like this one.

"Ooh, I'm gonna be so hot!" he said to himself over and over, as he took a shower in the marble tub.

Vicki freshened-up and changed into pink Bermuda shorts, along with a coordinating plaid sleeveless cotton top that she tucked into her waist high shorts. She thought beige sneakers and frilly white socks to be her footwear of the afternoon.

When Ben came out of the bathroom, he was drenched in cologne and had his hair combed completely back like a Chicago gangster, except for the one lock of hair that swept down his forehead and over his left eye. He put on his short-sleeved black spandex shirt that opened down to the beginnings of his chest hair region, then he squeezed into his tight, faded jeans. He then slipped into brown leather sandals that showed off his well-groomed feet.

Ben asked excitedly, "Ready, hon?"

They left their cabin for the evening.

A video crew was taking shots of passengers dancing, as the ship departed. Rum drinks were being sold to almost everyone partaking in the festivities. The couple was having a really great time, it seemed, just being together, staring into each others eyes, until that one tall blonde moment happened. The blondie with the roving eyes and riveting legs strolled by the couple's table.

Ben lost sight of Vicki, caught sight of "legs", and all bets were off. He told Vicki that he had to go back to the cabin to get his camera.

Vicki waited for close to twenty minutes, until she couldn't wait any longer. She got up from the table, after her third and final Margarita. She walked around the deck, trying to find the shortest way back to Ben and their cabin on the massive vessel.

To her amazement, there Ben was, having a drink with the tall blonde.

"Whatever, you dumb shit," was all that Vicki could vocalize. She felt like a fool that she had trusted him, enough to take him on this *love* cruise, and there he was acting like a playboy. She felt humiliated and naive.

She unlocked the cabin door and crawled into bed, crying the whole while, until she fell asleep. Two hours later, she was awakened by the touch of a hand on her face. The touch was Ben's.

He said "I'm so sorry Victoria. You know, I love you so. That girl meant nothing to me, and as a matter of fact, she told me that she only likes girls. She caught me as I was going past her table and said she thought she knew me from the University of Texas. I asked her what her name was, and she said, 'Kimberly Hatchett, from art class,' and so I sat and talked with her, and that is when you came walking by.

After you said what you did to me and stormed out, I left her table, took my drink and stood by the railing thinking of how much I love and need you in my life. Please believe me. You're all that I talked about to that girl," he assured her, as he finished his story. He then gave her a glass of water and a supposed aspirin and finished stroking her into unconsciousness.

The next morning came like a ray of sunshine. Vicki was pretty much satisfied with Ben's tale and ready to start the day with enthusiasm by the pool. They skipped breakfast, slipped on their bathing suits, and headed straight for the small, deep pool, where they both dived in, without testing the water.

Ben said that it felt exhilarating. They both played in the water together like children for about an hour, then stretched out their striped towels on sun chairs by the pool.

Ben said to Vicki, "Victoria, when we dock in Nassau this afternoon, why don't you take a short prop plane ride to Freeport and see a reality firm about property on that island? I hear it's hot there now, and a real deal. I'll meet you back at the airport, say in about six hours. Want to do this adventure for me? I mean for *us*. We could have a great life in the Bahamas and maybe still keep the house in the states," he murmured to her, not knowing what her response would be.

Vicki thought for a couple of minutes, then shot him a heavy, pensive glare, and immediately burst into laughter.

"Sure, why not? I mean we do only live once, and I'm ready for something different. The ticket is usually real cheap, and I've never seen the island. If the market is as hot and inexpensive as you say, well, you know I'm in the game. Let me put on a sundress and let the cruise desk take care of this reservation for me."

"The steward said that we'd be docking in about two hours, so there's plenty of time," Ben reassured her.

"Oh, I really do hope this works out for us. This is what we need!" Vicki exclaimed, with an underlying sense of overall fear.

Their sea-side bungalow in Honduras had been a fraud. Vicki had been scammed out of five thousand dollars, put down as a deposit. The *agent* did not answer his phone, after he received her check.

One week later, his phone had been disconnected. She then knew that she had been had.

"I guess it could have been worse," she said to herself. "But it won't happen again."

NINE

The Blunt

Vicki got on the prop with only a small wallet purse and a real estate magazine in her hand that she picked up at the pier in Nassau. Before she left, she called an agent in the magazine that had several possible properties and arranged an address to meet when she got in at three.

Vicki hailed a taxi at the Freeport airport when she cleared customs. The cabbie glared at her and took her to the address she had written down on the crumpled up piece of paper which she retrieved from her pocket. This was a house that appeared to be in bad need of repair, not the stunning picture shown in the magazine.

The taxi driver waited with her for twenty minutes. He was a nice Bahamian, probably around seventy, and he was too worried about this pretty woman's safety to just leave her in a strange place alone.

Finally he interrupted their silences with, "I don't think the person's comin', do you?"

"No, but let me call them first," she replied.

The phone number she dialed on her prepaid phone just rang and rang.

Vicki got disgusted, hung-up, and screamed, "Let's get the hell out of this dump. I'm tired of dealing with con artists and shady deals. Where can I go to that's fun, and in the sun?" she asked the taxi driver.

He stated, "Port Lucaya. There are bars, shops, boats and beaches. It's a good place for young people like you."

She simply smiled knowing she was now in her later thirties, and apprehensively staring at forty. The driver said to her that it would probably be hard to find a taxi back to the airport at that time of day. She told him that she would be fine.

At three-thirty she was dropped off at the port. She paid the driver generously for waiting with her and being a gentleman, of whom she hardly encounters nowadays. She walked up to a British style pub that was located in the shopping district across from the lavish homes on the beach. She ordered a Cosmopolitan, then another, and decided it was time for her to go. She had to be at the airport in an hour and a half to board her flight back to Nassau. She strolled around the shopping area, looking inside quaint shops of white, dressed up with blue and white striped awnings overhanging the front doors.

When Vicki finally arrived at the taxi-stand area, she found no one, and no taxis. Again, she waited for close to fifteen minutes.

"Well," she thought to herself, "It will be tough to get back."

She didn't know what to do now, and in a panic, she crossed the barren street for the beach.

Vicki began to jog up and down the almost-deserted stretch of beach, until she was stopped by a young Bahamian man who said, "What's the hurry? You've got to be happy and slow down. Why rush?"

Vicki answered, "I'm rushing, because I have to catch a plane back to Nassau in an hour, and there are no cabs."

"Is that all it is?" he smiled and winked at her. "I've got a nice car. I'll take you to the plane. Let's go."

She had no other choice at this point.

She thought, "I have a lot of my belongings and some jewelry on the ship. Ben's expecting me at a certain time, and how else would I get home, if not on the ship. I could get a plane ticket from Freeport back to the states and pick up my rental car in Orlando." "Ohhh….what a mess I've gotten myself into," she mumbled to herself.

"What did you say?" the Bahamian asked.

She said, "What are you waiting on? I'm ready to go."

They both walked up the sand dune and over to the street, where they found a beat up, maroon nineteen eighty-nine Toyota Corolla. The two sped off on a deserted two lane road, surrounded by pine trees… sheer desolation. She planned how she might exit the car if held hostage, while speeding down the road. She squeezed into the corner of her torn fabric seat, waiting for any given moment the sense to open the door and roll out onto the long, but manicured fresh grass which lined the lonely highway.

Instead, he pulled into the driveway of a small, but tidy house. It stood alone, in a mass of tall pine trees. He got out of the car, slammed the door, and shouted through the open window, "I'll be right back."

Vicki wanted to leave the car, but knew that she was so far off the beaten path now that she could never find her way to civilization. So she stayed, hoping.....praying.

As she closed her eyes to give her last solemn oath of all the good she would do on this planet if she got out of this situation unscathed, she heard the car door unlatch. The Bahamian frantically hopped inside and cranked up the engine.

Vicki opened her eyes and screamed, "What's going on?" The car screeched out of the drive.

"It was a set-up. The buyers inside called their boys just as I was leaving and tried to wrestle me down to the ground. I kicked them both in the nuts, punched them in the esophagus, I fled the dump, and here I am. Their boys are on the way here. They're on the lookout for this tin can, so let's get to the airport fast. By the way, my name is Gerald.... and you?"

"I'm Victoria. What do you mean by set-up?" she asked Gerald.

"It's drugs....all kinds of them. The deal at that house went sour. That happens sometimes. I have a blunt, if that will soothe your nerves." He calmly turned into the small airport's entrance, as he put the marijuana filled cigar in his mouth over and over again, until they reached the departure terminal.

She nervously climbed out of his car, stuttered "Ththanks" and "Googood-luluck" and ran into the airport to board the plane to Nassau, back to Ben, back to safety, back to looking forward to their great future. She thought about this horrifying experience all the way back to Nassau, about how she could have been held as an accomplice, just for being at the wrong place at the wrong time. She vowed never ever to get involved in a whimsical situation like that ever again. She always needed to think things through first.

Since she had met Ben, however, it seemed like her pretty solidly-planted common sense had been uprooted, and now she was on a dare-devil course.

Walking from the plane into the gate area, she noticed a young man's body running down the long hall. He was coming toward her on the right. The closer he got to her focal range, the more she thought he looked like Ben. Then, she heard her name, and she knew that it was him.

"What was he doing?" she thought to herself. She was supposed to take a taxi back to the ship to meet him at six thirty just in time for their farewell dinner celebration.

She noticed he had tears in his lifeless eyes, as he approached her saying, "Baby, I love you so much. I missed you so much. I was worried about you. I should have never let you go there by yourself. Anything could have happened."

"And it did," she angrily scolded him.

Vicki told him about the whole episode, then took Ben in her arms and started bawling, dripping out all her fears and anxieties. Ben limply held her, dried off the wet from under his suddenly glistening eyes, and smiled devilishly, as he spied on a tanned white-haired forty-year old who wore sunglasses, a tube top, and a very short mini skirt. He knew she had money because of her authentic jewel assortment around her neck, fingers and toes.

Vicki felt like a teenager in love. She knew how much he truly cared for her, after this display of his emotions.

"I'm so lucky, and so in love," she sexily whispered in his ear.

He stroked Vicki's hair, looking for the hot miniskirt, which had almost showed him the girl's entire package.

He told Vicki, "Everything's perfect. I'm here whenever you need me."

His eyes finally met the skirt's eyes. The skirt's eyes winked at Ben, and Ben returned the greeting, watching as she walked off, holding her skirt in such a way that he could view a little of her bare bottom.

He remained in this mystery woman's sexual spell, until he put his hand in his back jean short's pocket. His stuff was gone.

He went into a panic and started scouring garbage cans, searching counters and carpeting. Then he realized. The stuff must have been snatched by one of the two broads that he had just become intimate with on the ship. He knew he had to have his weed to emotionally get through the rest of the trip. He couldn't play the "good boy" for the remaining day and a half without the weed, nor the *knockout pills.*

And so the pendulum swings…

TEN

THE CHARADE

The short bird ride had seemed an eternity, as that rerun of insanity played over and over again in her now fragile mind. She didn't even know that there had been anyone sitting beside her, trying to talk to her. She had not heard a sound, not even when the puddle jumper skidded on the runway.

She didn't come back to reality until the short, stout male flight attendant had touched her shoulder and whispered in a British accent, "We've landed. It's time to leave the plane."

Vicki had slowly retrieved her belongings and ran down the aisle, then down the movable stairway, onto the runway, then into the terminal. On the other side of the glass entrance, she had seen Ben running, struggling to get through the waiting crowd. When he first saw Vicki, he cried and ran to greet her with open arms.

"I had to get here before that taxi driver or his cohorts got here to pick you up. I know they had plenty of mischief on their minds. They told me. Please, never leave me again. This was a stupid, stupid idea! Well, let's have a great rest of the cruise, and remember…I love you so much." Vicki smiled and didn't utter a word the whole peaceful taxi ride back.

That evening, Vicki slept like a baby, never even waking to go to dinner. When she finally did awaken five hours later, however, Ben was nowhere in the cabin. She didn't care. She was so exhausted and sick of the charade. Tomorrow, she would be in Orlando, heading back in her rental car for home!

"Oh, yeah," she sarcastically thought, "with my faithful, 'til death do us part boyfriend." She remembered him saying that to her once.

She sank back into an unconsciousness that lasted another nine hours. She finally was awakened by several banging fists on her cabin door.

She screamed, "What the hell?" and looked at her watch. It was eight-thirty and the sun was beaming in through her tightly drawn thick, white curtains. Two stewards unlocked her cabin door, looked inside, and helped Vicki out of the bed. She did not seem able to by herself. Her head was heavy, and it hurt so much that she couldn't even see straight.

"What happened to me?" she asked the steward perplexed.

One of them answered, "You must have had too much to drink last night, but don't worry, you'll be alright. Now, we'll leave you to get dressed. Shout when you're done and we'll disembark with you."

She threw on a tight black work-out jumpsuit, sneakers, grabbed her purse, packed her duffel and met the stewards outside her door. She carefully walked down the gangway, with hands placed firmly on the railing for balance. She never even thought or cared of where her "beloved" might be.

"Well, just leave me, why don't ya?" she heard an angry voice off in the distance.

She continued walking, not knowing or caring to where. Out of the corner of her squinting, sun-scorched retina, she saw a topless, muscular "blue-jeaned" body about to side-swipe her. Vicki immediately jumped up and backed out of the way of the body. The body was Ben's.

He grabbed her neck, shook her several times, yelling words of angst, then he broke into tears.

"Where were you all night?" she asked sternly, but quietly.

Ben started sobbing even more upon hearing this question.

He remained silent, wiping away his tears, until a flash of mischievous confidence darted through his eyes, and so he answered, "I was out on the deck thinking of us all night long and how I really don't deserve you. I was hoping and praying that I would have enough guts to ask you to stay with me. I mean forever. Let's get our heads on with work and money issues and maybe we can get married some-day, how 'bout it?"

Vicki sheepishly muttered, "Sure."

She didn't want any more turmoil. She simply wanted a peaceful ride back home. Then, she would think about what was to come. Her headache was now almost completely gone, and she was able to stand without dropping over.

"What happened last night?" she asked herself.

All she knew was that she still didn't feel like herself and couldn't think entirely straight. She had never done drugs but imagined it would have the same feeling.

The ride home from the pier was uneventful. All that the two of them did was listen to the radio, never talking. Upon pulling into the carport at the top of the hill, Ben got out of the car and made his way to the other side of the vehicle to open the door for "His Lady".

"This is very unusual. He has never done this before. Maybe he *is* changing," Vicki hoped, full of hopeless naivety.

The travel agency was bustling with clients, even though the Airline Reporting Corporation had stopped paying commissions to agencies. *Leisure Days* had a negotiated deal with several of the major airlines, however, and they received a percentage of the ticket. This agency handled four universities, a huge and profitable reality company in the area, and all of the governmental and military forces in the state. Obviously, it had the power to negotiate commissions in its realm.

Long, busy days with not enough pay was all that she could think of when she got home every night. Ben was starving all the time, so she had to buy large amounts of groceries, with large amounts of dollars being strewn on one of her many almost maxed-out credit cards. She had no cash on her person, only bills in her purse that she struggled to pay daily.

"How can I continue to live this way? I know I should be able to, but I'm so tired," she blurted out to herself, as she drove like a robot to work one dreary morning.

Back at the home front, Ben was making phone calls, in between his drags of ghetto-grown weed, trying to show he was making an effort, but never following through. When the going got tough, Ben always got lazy. On one of their first dates, while playing charades, Ben had pulled out a joint. Vicki stared horridly at him after doing so. Ben stated that he had never smoked a joint before this one. "My friend gave me one this afternoon, so why not?" he sullenly asked.

Vicki now realized that he was addicted to marijuana. As unbelievable as it seemed to her, living with this seemingly addicted pot-smoking man was far worse than living with an alcoholic, like her ex-husband had become. She now realized that Ben had to get his fix on a daily basis. If he didn't get it, he would go ballistic. HE HAD TO HAVE HIS WEED, HOURLY.

One night he went to the "hood" at two in the morning to see if he could find it, after first pleading with Vicki to loan him thirty. He said he would pay it back to her next week and said that he was scheduled to do a small faux-finishing job. She had no choice but to give it to him, to make him happy and to get him out of his maniacal state. She felt doomed and all used up. She loved him so, and yet now hated him so.

Financially, Vicki was sinking fast. Her savings was going, and she was not bringing home a fat enough pay check for Ben's growing needs for drugs. He would be cool for a week, then go crazy trying to find a stash. He seemed now to be struggling a bit to stay in this game.

Ben was helping a small bit, like buying groceries, paying a utility bill, and buying knickknacks, from time to time. This helped Vicki, but it wasn't enough. She knew she had to complete her master's, so that she could earn more *mula*, and so she re-enrolled at her hometown university.

Vicki registered for three graduate courses in education which she scheduled starting at six in the evening, three nights a week. She mustered up enough strength to do well for the first month.

One night, at the end of this first month, Vicki got home later than usual, as she had to stop at the university library to check-out an instructional reading. Vicki didn't call Ben to tell him she would be a little late, because her cell phone battery was dead.

"No big deal. He'll be okay," she muttered to herself, as she unlocked the car door.

When she pulled around the bend, she peered up into the carport and saw nothing, no jeep. Ben was not there.

She suddenly got an eerie feeling, as she flung open the screen door and stumbled inside, throwing down her books on the tiled floor.

She cried, "Ben….Ben," as she ran through the hall towards their bedroom.

It was in the bedroom that she became stupefied.

On the ornate glass mirror, above the large mahogany desk, smeared in red lipstick were the words, ***I loved you whore***.

ELEVEN

Mr. Hyde

As she sat at the laundromat near the couple's abode, she listened to the squawking of plump doves, the rustling of leaves in the brisk wind, and the cranking-up of motor boat engines docked across the street in the lake marina. Vicki felt how truly blessed she was to have endured her past marriage and come out shining like a "star", in her estimation.

"I am the luckiest woman on this planet to have a new man like I do," she shouted into the empty street. "I love my life! And I can't wait to put in a washer and dryer combo of my own!" She wondered when, or if that would ever happen.

After this sudden burst of optimism and joy, Vicki sullenly walked back into the laundromat only to find a picture of her lovely white, two-story countrified house that was for sale, and which was being advertised on the bulletin board in the laundromat.

She loved the way it looked, and she put her finger on the house, as if she wanted to touch it.

She never got over the loss of this house that she had poured so much of her love, trust and MONEY into. Her heart saddened with the memory of desire, lust and pain. Sometimes, she thought, love and hate become so intertwined. When they come together at the end of each spectrum, as too much love and too much hate, each emotion seems to blend into one. "These are two very similar emotions," she whispered to herself.

All that really mattered now, however, was that they were moving to Florida to start their new life.

"Excess is bad in every venue. Moderation is the key to success," she repeated the words of her ex-husband, Richard. He was a very entertaining, but sarcastic mate, who turned out to be only creative in thought, unfortunately, not in creating money, or kids, and he never wanted to adopt.

"No children," he changed his tune, soon after they took their vows. "I had my three, and now I want to have fun. No children, so if you still want kids, find a younger man."

She took his advice, and the uncontested divorce was granted four years later.

As her clothes were drying, she began to drift back, back to sweet serenity, the only serenity that Ben and Vicki shared together. It was only at the beginning.

Vicki had been a trusting soul, a school teacher by trade, wanting to alleviate the troubles of the world. She met up with mysterious Ben, and all bets are off. With great looks, and even greater charm and finesse, Ben hit Vicki's heart like a sledgehammer. She had been knocked off her socks. Ben was so wonderful at first, wining and dining her, and of course, saying all of the perfect things. The few hours that they spent together every night for the first three months were heavenly to her.

She had never met a young man like him, he being eleven years her junior.

He never had a mother of which to speak, so he fell for her head first, not for beauty and appeal, but for her slight sexiness, and her parental ability to hold down the fort, and for her money, of which she really had very little, as her inheritance had been virtually none. Her parents had lost most of the family's money in loans to now bankrupt clientele.

Her sweet, serene memories were now quickly fading and were slowly being replaced with memories of intense sadness, regret, and resentment.

Ben thought Vicki had a lot of assets and cash, for whatever reason. Maybe, because of the supreme way she carried herself, her tenaciousness, and for her ability to make people like her. Ben thought that these were qualities of wealth, and that they were to make him aspire to greatness, or so he thought. He was very talented, yet very lazy and unorganized, very unenthusiastic, and *very*, *very mentally weak*

He just wanted to be taken care of...and guided through life, having plenty of money in hand...and if he didn't get everything he wanted, all hell repeatedly broke loose.

Her serene state had vanished completely, as she remembered the rest.

Once married, Ben slowly turned into a "Mr. Hyde", as he built their dream house, slower, then slower, as he knew most of the materials for the project were put on her credit cards...with the promise of paying them off by the bank, as soon as the house was completed which *had to be* within six months. Time was of the essence for Ben. He knew that he could not let it happen that quickly, not if he wanted to cash in on his plan. He needed and wanted to bleed her dry, never thinking or caring about tomorrow. He was vengeful and jealous, as well, and he loved to see Vicki struggle. He also loved to fight, mentally and physically...and win.

Ben knew he could do and ask for whatever he so desired...mostly with her financial future being in jeopardy, along with his insurance of possessing a brutally forceful fist, so he never actually had to work, which he couldn't and wouldn't anyway, not without the vices which eventually led to his demise.

Ben refused to work, in order to meet his daily deadlines of construction, until she would give him enough money for the drugs to satisfy his addiction. Vicki always caved into his demands, giving him whatever he wanted and needed. She became more strapped for cash every single day.

She began tutoring at the end of her work day to help pay for his needs and even turned to becoming an "escort", so she could make the money that might enable him to finish her growing money pit building project. She was becoming a very tired and frightened young woman at the age of thirty-seven.

She was now a frustrated workhorse, who had no life of her own and was totally dominated by her mentally cruel and violent, drug-addicted spouse, who didn't have the capability of channeling his creativity, of which he had plenty, and of which he used for both commendable and criminal activities.

In addition, he was only a fair poet, which he had always aspired to be, but he was a genius at engineering and architecture, which he came by naturally. His late grandfather had been the master electrical engineer at the large air-conditioning facility in Collierville.

One evening Ben noticed that Vicki did not show enough money in her checking register, and therefore could not give him any money to buy his daily bag of weed. Ben stood up on one of the sturdy kitchen dinette chairs and started pulling out pieces from the delicate chandelier of which he had just diligently installed, twisting and disfiguring them with some sort of steel instrument.

"Stop it! You ARE crazy. You just put that up!" she screamed.

"Yeah, and I guess you are going to have to get a REAL electrical man, and a brand new window," he laughed, as he picked up a coffee cup and threw it at the newly installed bay window. It made a horrifying sound in the silent night.

Vicki sat in the corner on the floor and cried her eyes out.

She screamed, "I am doomed."

Her husband stormed out of the house. He did not return until morning, all drugged-up.

"You are so disgusting," Vicki pronounced.

"Maybe, but at least I'm high," he cunningly smiled.

Ben loved to cause misery and hurt to others. Victoria thought about how psychologically damaged she discovered that he was soon after they were married, and how he seemed to possess no conscious whatsoever. Most manic depressives that she had met in the past seemed that way also, but only at particular times. For Benjamin, however, it was perpetual.

TWELVE

THE TRAILER

Ben told Vicki about an acre and a half of land that was for sale in northern Mississippi, south of Collierville. He said that he saw it as he was driving around, upon leaving his grandmother's house and saw this land that also had a large pond on it.

Later that week, they both drove out to take a look at it. Vicki seemed to like it and called the owner to discuss the terms. She still had some change from her divorce settlement, and she was the idea of living in the countryside really appealed to her. She had always lived in the city, so she was looking forward to peace and quiet, even though that would mean a much longer commute to work for her, and to shop for anything, even groceries would be a feat. To see any of her friends, or go out to dinner, would be very infrequent events.

"Oh well," she sighed. I'll use a lot more gasoline, but still save, because property taxes here are so much lower here."

Thinking of that angle, she called the owner back to arrange a time and place where a contract could be signed.

Later that evening, the three met at a popular pub in the city to have a beer, write a check and sign a contract. The property was then Vicki's officially, so the couple drove back to their house, picked up a raft, and drove out to the parcel. Ben threw the raft in the pond, tied it up to a small tree and proceeded to get into it, dragging his kicking, screaming and laughing wife all the while. They fell asleep under the stars and the cool April breeze and awoke to the most beautiful sunrise either one had ever seen.

They were married four months prior in Gatlinburg, Tennessee in a snow-covered wedding chapel. They rented a cabin in the hills for the weekend, equipped, with a hot tub on their private deck. It was a fun-filled weekend for the two of them. She had purchased a beautiful off-white, laced wedding dress, and he rented a tux for the big event.

They had actually driven up to the hills of Pennsylvania, two weeks earlier, in order to have an impromptu wedding ceremony in the town where her father was born. While there, they found it to be impossible to get married, because they could not get a license issued, nor a justice of the peace to come to where they were staying. This was due to the blizzard that set in after they had arrived.

Vicki had to get back to work on Tuesday, so they left when the storm had lessened. Ben sped most of the way home.

When they got home, they planned a time and place, when and where they could get married. They both decided on two weeks from that day at a small chapel in Gatlinburg. Then Vicki informed the minister that she wanted to keep her maiden name. Ben grimaced.

On her lunch break the next day, she called several chapels and cabin rentals until she found the right ones that were available and perfect, while not being too pricey. Vicki reserved each, and they left two weeks later, again in snow, but which was not threatening this time.

One week before, Ben had acquired a customer relations job with a big firm through an employment agency. Things were finally looking up. Vicki was psyched.

Soon after the acquisition of the property four months earlier, Ben was fired from the firm. Victoria needed to buy a small used trailer with cooking facilities where they could stay during the building of the house. She had to use her own money for the purchase. Ben, she found out, never saved. For the four months in which he was employed, he did not have a dime to his name to show for his earnings.

When Vicki quickly sold her house without an agent, she paid off credit cards and set some cash aside. This came in handy to purchase the needed trailer. She also needed money for their five dogs' vet appointments and for their soon to be second puppy litter.

Their first one came at their former house in Memphis, when Ben captured a dog that was thrown out of a car coming down the street. "Bethany" ended up having two adorable puppies, who were later given away to a utility worker who helped with the building of the house.

Two months afterward, Vicki asked him how the puppies were doing. He informed her that they had run away, but assured her that they were fine. Looking as happy and assured with this new development as he did, Vicki knew that he had sold the beautiful Chows for a big price.

When the second litter of five arrived, underneath the trailer in October, Vicki tended to them like the puppies were her own children. Her motherly instincts were now at an all-time high, especially with her youth beginning to fade.

Ben also wanted children badly. So, he included a changing room, beside the laundry room, in his secret architectural renderings that he let no one view but himself. The only problem with starting this family was how they were to survive. Who was going to make money rearing children and going through pregnancies? And Ben's obsessive use of marijuana would have to go, and she knew that he would or could never stop.

Now, however, the main thing that Vicki was concentrating on was how to get more financial help. Most of her money had been put into the home-building fund, which dwindled away with each phase and had gone to settle the loan for the purchase of her land. She made known her concerns daily with Ben. So, their fighting sessions started and continued on a daily basis. Tempers also began to fly with the crew who was laying the foundation.

One day, Ben took out his grandfather's unloaded shotgun and started running after one of the workers, who he affirmed was not doing his job right. The workers ran to their truck, got in and never returned to finish. Vicki had paid them half up front, and they had not yet completed half of the foundation work. This episode started the beginning of the end with her finances, and her marriage.

Ben started hiring poorly-qualified workers to begin building the house. He would tell Vicki the estimates given by workers on each facet of building. She always thought the prices to be decent enough, so she would give Ben the cash to pay each set of contractors and workers. Ben would give the builders three-quarters of the proceeds and keep the rest for himself. With all these commitments, his stress was growing, and so was his drug use.

Upon coming home from work early one day, she found a startled Ben running out to her car to meet her. Vicki looked up towards her trailer, anxious to get inside to change her clothes, and there was a big empty spot on the land. The trailer was gone.

Screaming, she started tearing at his hair, asking where the trailer that she bought was. Vicki was beginning to feel out of control with her emotions. She was supposed to sell the trailer back to the previous owner as soon as the house was fit to live in, for half the price. This, she was looking forward to, as she was beginning to desperately need the money. The trailer, however, was gone now. Ben had sold it. He said he sold it to pay a bill.

When Vicki looked inside his jeep, however, she found bags and bags of marijuana, so she knew what the money went toward. She also pulled out notes and pictures that he had strewn on top of the seats. Written below each photo was Ben's level of prospect for each candidate.

She gasped. He was now making money as a gigolo! He had not given her a cent for two months. She packed up her puppies and clothing, which were now inside the partially framed structure, and left for her aunt's and uncle's home up the way. She hoped that Ben was responsible enough to at least take care of the five grown dogs during her absence.

THIRTEEN

HELD FOR RANSOM

She was welcomed wholeheartedly at her uncle's home. Her aunt carried the puppies that Vicki gave her in a warm, fuzzy blanket and laid that same blanket underneath the pups in their screened-in porch. It was still cool enough outside for the puppies to feel comfortable. Vicki's uncle said that he was glad she had come to stay with them.

"I never liked the guy to begin with," her uncle confessed. She grinned and tiredly walked back to the guest room.

As she climbed into her bed, she then realized that she must cater to Ben's every demand, if she ever wanted to see her home finished. Since unstable Ben had all of the building plans of the work in progress, she wondered if she would ever again have light, air, heat and a stove. She was tired of sleeping in ninety-five degree temperatures in the summer and zero degree readings in winter. She was tired of heating her canned foods on a single pot burner in the dark. She felt like she was being held for ransom.

She had to do something, but what, she knew not. Years ago, she had been given almost eighty thousand dollars for an accident in which an underage driver was consuming alcohol at a local restaurant where she worked at the time. He drove her almost to her death. The chain restaurant settled out of court, and Vicki felt satisfied with the amount.

She had never let any of her dwindling money out of her sight…that was until slick Ben entered the picture and fulfilled her fantasy…what turned out to be a demonic fantasy that she had to *endure* for five years, until she got pay back….and lots of it.

Ben, along with his occasional male or female thug cohort, were simply bullies. Some of the moments she tragically remembered included a simple Super Bowl Sunday outing which turned into a horrific beating session at their former house where blood stains adorned the walls. He had flown into a jealous rage, when a sheriff's deputy who was at the party paid a little too much attention to Vicki, in Ben's estimation.

Ben injured Vicki both emotionally and physically. She had a terribly swollen nose, and an injured hip and arm. She never told anyone he was to blame.

Ben promised to get much needed help, but of course never did, and his rage got more and more out of control.

Another insane scene took place later on, near where their house was being constructed, out in the country in a sparsely populated trailer park, where Ben asked Vicki to meet him one night to bring him money to buy a tool for a project in the house.

When she got there, she saw six horribly scary men who quickly surrounded her SUV. Ben asked Vicki to climb out so that the guys could see how pretty she was. She rolled up her window and put her vehicle in reverse and peeled out of the gravel road. At that moment, she knew that Ben, in his demented mind, must have wanted her brutally raped, perhaps even killed. Vicki more and more began to break out of her naive shell.

Ben had someone call her school, pretending to be Vicki. The impersonator gave Vicki's social security number and got into the automated system, leaving false information about sick days and making unprofessional comments on the message at the same time. She was written up for her remarks and lack of leadership. She could not prove that it wasn't her.

So, when Vicki arrived at the construction site several months later, after a long day of testing, and was greeted by large tire tracks which lead to a vacant space once belonging to their make-shift abode of a trailer, she knew that she was being had. He obviously had been using her since the beginning. The trailer was gone, because once again, Ben said he needed some money. They were then forced to begin their one year stint without air or heat, only one lamp, only one burner, and only one mattress with six dogs for warmth in the cold months. It was sheer misery and hell, living only in a framed house with no drywall.

Looking at her bank statements one morning, she noticed that her balance didn't add up. She checked all deposits and checks cashed and noticed there were several fifty dollar checks that she evidently never recorded…that was because she never wrote them. Ben did, and forged her signature. This caused her to have bounced checks and fees for every check she had written for a whole month, which had been numerous.

It had been all too much for her, so when she read in the local rag about a better paying job being offered in St. Petersburg, she excitedly faxed her resume at the hotel desk.

FOURTEEN

THE MANGE

Through all the fighting and frantic episodes where Ben called and drove around maniacally until he found a fix, the couple managed to have most necessities installed in their money pit during the year after framing, except for one important one, the toilet. There was one working shower and a sink in the kitchen, enough to get by for a while. This was all accomplished because of Vicki using professionals, not Ben.

"You don't need to call a plumber to install it," he advised her. "I'm getting around to it."

"I am calling a local plumber here in Mississippi. I cannot and WILL not live like this anymore."

The portable toilet that she had rented for over ten months was scheduled to be picked-up the next day. She was doing everything she could in order to cut costs. She was even discussing bankruptcy with an attorney. She couldn't pay her credit cards and certificate of deposit loans, so she just stopped paying them on a regular basis, only when she was able to.

After the six months that were allotted by the bank to build the house, so there would be enough equity to obtain a loan, her credit score plummeted. Everything up until had been put on her credit cards, and she was maxed out.

Months before, Victoria was advised that she would not be offered a loan to pay for the property and house, not because she did not have an excellent credit score, but because the home was not to be built by a licensed contractor.

"If you want to save and build yourself, you won't be able to get a loan," her banker told her. "You can, however, put your savings in CD's and pay against them every month like a loan."

"What happens if I skip a month?" Vicki questioned the associate.

"It is the same thing as a loan, like I said. If you skip a month, you will be charged a late fee. However, it won't go against your credit, because you are paying off your own money. Do you understand?" he asked.

"Now I do, yes," she clarified.

"The only way you can lose with this option is if you don't pay anything against it.

When we loan money against a certificate of deposit, and it is not paid back, we freeze the CD, and it becomes property of the bank," he explained.

"Well, it seems like my only option, and the interest rate is good, so let's do it," she asserted, hesitantly.

"Okay, I'll have the papers drawn up and we can settle it here tomorrow."

"In the morning, say around ten? I am anxious to get this money to start paying off some of my credit cards that I have put mortar, cement, wood, and paint, and more on. I am really desperate. Thank you so, so much," she giggled, easing her way out of the office.

"I will be here at nine, so ten is fine. See you tomorrow," the bank officer replied.

Driving back to her half-finished abode, she wondered if she was doing the right thing putting her savings at risk, and how was she going to pay all of the credit cards debts that had already accrued, with so many more to come.

The loan went through the next day. Victoria got her money which helped the situation a little.

For the next week, Vicki's husband was almost a ghost on the property. He had supposed business deals in other counties, but he never came home with any money.

Then one night, she found out why he had vacated the residence.

They were sleeping on a mattress on the unvarnished wood floor. It was a nice October night, so the windows were open. They were both waked-up by high-beam headlights and a race engine sounding vehicle in their back yard. Ben got up immediately and flew down the stairs, and went outside, yelling curse words all the while. It was too late, however. His jeep was gone. It was not stolen, however, but repossessed by the small auto dealership that sold it to him in the first place.

"I am good and pissed," he angrily stomped the hard ground in the back of the yard.

"You have not been paying for the jeep? What is the matter with you? Why didn't you tell me?" she interrogated Ben.

"Should I have? You wouldn't help me pay for the jeep anyway. You don't help me with anything. All you care about is yourself and keeping all the money to yourself," he said, starring at her, with venom coming from his eyes, ears, and mouth.

"What money? The little that I had was gone the minute I bought the land and put down the foundation. I have been using credit for all the supplies. That is why I need YOU to help me finish the house, not workers. There is no more money in my account."

"Oh yeah, then how did you get that loan from the bank if you don't have no money?"

"I had a couple of small CD's. I received two loans against them. I have to pay on these CD's every month. It's like having two loans, plus all of the credit card debt I have. In order to pay for the guys you hire when you are too lazy or high to work to be paid, I have to now work tutoring jobs throughout the county, at night, starting next week. Real fun for me, huh, having to work my life away to pay for a boy that sits and gets high all day and won't finish building, because I don't have the money to subsidize his wants and needs. That is like a form of *domestic ransom*. Do you hear that?" and she violently started pounding his chest.

He shoved her against the living room wall and held his hand around her scrawny neck to where Vicki could not make a sound. He was a pro. She could tell he had done this kind of thing many times before, most likely when he was out of weed, which he was at that moment.

Ben let go of his wife's neck and spit at her face.

He walked out of the house, toward the convenience store.

Vicki was glad he had, as she was fearful of her life at that moment. She slept in that front room, with her large brown *mut*, who resembled a police dog, right by her side.

Her dog was beginning to get the chills, so he curled up super close to her. She could tell something was terribly wrong when she pulled out a clump of dry hair from his back, as she was stroking him.

FIFTEEN

The Loan

The next day came and went. Ben had vanished. Nobody knew where he had gone. Nobody seemed like they really cared. Vicki couldn't take it any longer. She hired a plumbing company in the next town to come over to the country and install the toilet, sink, and shower. She couldn't and wouldn't bathe in a bathing suit with hose water plummeting over her head any longer.

While sitting at the breakfast table one morning, feeling rather glad that her husband had given her some space. She really needed the breathing room to think, relax, and get her head together. Vicki knew that he would come stumbling home one day. He always did. He was starting to do these types of things on a regular basis. She amazed herself that it didn't bother her, not knowing where her husband was, or who he was with. When the going got tough in any way, he got going. He always left the scene, never facing reality. Her respect for the man had all but dried up, not that she really had that much in the first place. She just liked his looks and the feeling she got when she looked his way.

She picked up an old magazine that was lying in a box in the laundry area. Thumbing through the pages, she came upon an ad stating "Hard-ship loans. No one is denied."

She picked up the phone and excitedly pushed in the numbers. A young girl's voice answered. Vicki relayed to her the ad she had seen in the magazine, and she quickly connected her to a gentleman. She told this loan officer her situation in detail, while sipping on a cup of mild Italian brew. He told her what documents she needed to gather up for him, income verifications, tax documents, and statements related to the building. These amounts would be paid off from the loan.

"Send them to me express, so that I can begin the process. I will then need to come to your house and evaluate its worthiness and take pictures for our file. I will then tell you the interest rate and terms that we can offer you. Sound fair?" the gentleman asked Vicki.

"It does. When can you come to do this? I really want to get this show on the road. I have so many people that I want and need to pay off," she stressed harshly in a shrill voice.

"Well, I won't be able to come until next week sometime. I need that time to put the loan together, and besides, I have home value appointments scheduled every day until then," he clarified.

"So, you will just call me when you're ready for me?" she wondered.

"Yeah, and I should know the date and time in a couple of days," he declared.

"Sounds good," she answered.

"I will talk to you then," and he hung up the phone.

Just at that moment, Ben banged open the door, displaying a huge black and purple mark over his nose, continuing to his right cheek.

"What happened?" Vicki screamed.

Ben could barely get the words out of this mouth, and he stumbled down to the floor, "I was in a fight, got beat up. Give me some water, hurry."

She ran to get him a glass of water. Spilling a little of it, she pressed the glass to his lips.

Almost whispering, after he got his breath, he continued with his episode. She didn't know if it was made-up or not. It seemed so exaggerated.

"A big football player from that college in Collierville got drunk and started calling a girl at this party all kinds of names. I couldn't take hearing it, so I belted him in the stomach, until he stopped. Well, he got really mad and lunged toward me. He got me on the ground. He was so heavy that I couldn't move, and yes, I had had a few. He just started socking me in the face, so here you have it," he said, pointing to the damaged side of his face.

"Whatever," she cried out. "Couldn't you think of a better one than that, and you never called me? Where did you stay for all of these nights? What is going on here? I demand to know. You haven't done a darn thing to this house in weeks. I am so disgusted with you. When you are able, come here. I want to show you something."

He struggled to rise himself off the floor. When he finally did so, he followed her into the half bath.

She pointed to the toilet and vanity.

"I was going to do this. Why did you spend our money on this? Dumb, dumb, dumb. I really need some shit now to calm my nerves, and you probably don't have any money now, right?"

"Oh, you are so right," Vicki angrily affirmed.

Ben opened her bedroom closet door and pulled out her jewelry box that she had placed on the upper shelf. He rummaged through it and pulled out a couple of rings. He went out the side bedroom French door, climbing into a strange car she had never seen before, and he peeled out of the gravel drive.

She opened her jewelry box, only to find her favorite topaz ring, accented with diamonds, was gone, along with a child's junk jewelry ring from her youth.

Vicki was infuriated that he would dare go through his wife's belongs and steal them.

"Hey, you know whatever is yours is mine now," he shouted one night, when he was drunk, after building a camp fire to cook their dinner.

They had just moved into the framed house after Ben sold their trailer. They had no electricity for many months, only a generator that was loaned to them by a neighbor from time to time. It was like Vicki and Ben were living off the land. They had no comforts while building this house, but more importantly, they did not even have bare necessities. She felt she could not live like this another minute, but what was she to do?

Vicki had taken a huge chance with this project, and this man. She couldn't hire a contracting company to finish it out. She had no money for an expense such as that. The budget and time frame had been set in detail, months before the project got started. Neither one had been met. Her husband was bleeding her dry. He knew she had no other option now.

He appeared happy every time Vicki expounded on her financial difficulties. Ben did not know how much money she had left, but he hoped not enough to hire a crew to complete the project. In this way, he could bleed her dry, every month. Being in the middle of this struggle, he knew that she would *always have enough* to give him to satisfy his lifestyle.

She was a workaholic, like her father, and always managed to round-up enough money to get by. That was why he picked her out of the crowd. He asked members at the gallery about Vicki. A couple socialites told him what they knew of her, and he went in for the kill. The first prerequisite was that she was from the "right" zip code in Memphis. He knew from the start that with this older woman, he was going to live life like a king, having everything he ever wanted, drugs, women, cars, trips, and a place to dwell.

"I won't finish her house by the time the bank wants it done," he said to himself, "not if I want my plan to work. I have to put her through hell, so she's got to give me whatever I want."

The loan officer phoned Vicki later on in the after-noon and advised her that he needed the final build-ing permit to be faxed or sent to him, before he could get started.

The next morning Vicki called the county inspector to come out to the house for its final inspection. Ben had given her this phone number to use when he told her to schedule the inspection. She had not waited, however. The man who gruffly answered said the first opening he had was two days later, at eleven in the morning. She said that would be fine, and she waited patiently for the inspection to be completed, for her loan to be finalized, and for her husband to return home again.

The phone rang the next morning. Vicki wearily answered it.

"Hey, Vicki. Sorry I've been gone so long from home, but I needed a break. I am so stressed out that my mind is not working right, as far as my build-ing is concerned."

Vicki said nothing to her husband.

Finally, she uttered, "We will have our final inspection tomorrow."

Hysterical, Ben screamed, "No, you shouldn't have. It's not ready and will never pass. What's the inspector's name? What number did you call?"

She did not answer him, just hung-up the kitchen phone and went into the bedroom to look for county divorce attorneys online. She wrote down several numbers, then headed to work.

After work, she quickly drove home, so that she could take a hot Jacuzzi bath and sip a tall glass of full-bodied red wine. As soon as she was settled in the tub, the phone rang. She climbed out, wringing wet, to answer the ringing.

"Hi again. I know you are mad, but I can explain. Hey, can you meet me at a trailer park down the road at Byhalia and McAllister? I need you to bring me a tool that I need to finish a good paying job that I have here, right now."

She hopped into her sports car, without the tool, and headed to the spot he mentioned. Vicki wanted to give him a *piece of her mind.* She saw him at the end of the cove, standing with numerous darkish, heavy-set boys around him.

"Come on out honey. I want these boys to see how pretty you are," he said to her once again.

"No way," Vicki said, as she screeched her wheels out of the small gravel drive at the end of the cove, and she raced back home.

It was at this point that she believed he wanted her dead. She thought that if she had stepped out of that vehicle, she would have been killed for sure by those thugs.

Seconds after she arrived at her abode and entered through the quaint doorway off the front porch, furnished with white rocking chairs, she was met by Ben. He had followed her back. He was frantic.

"Honey, I love you. Why did you leave? I needed that tool."

He never said anything else about those thugs again. He was worried.

Vicki did not know if she were overreacting, but her intuition felt right. She had to divorce him, even though so much money would be lost. The house was not even near being ready to be sold, and she had gone way over budget due to Ben.

Ben laid in the bed with his wife for the entire night, eyes open, hardly blinking, just planning. He knew he had to damage something, so that the house would not pass a *real* final, if that is what it was to be. That way, he would still be able to have his weed for a little while longer. He made some calls. There was no answer, so he got no needed information.

Ben did not think much about the future. He had an addiction, so he lived day to day, hour to hour, and his manic depression even made his addiction worse. He raised from his slumber state and started pulling apart the drain pipes in the kitchen and rummaging through the insulation on the walls. Then he made a quick, whispered call.

He smiled, "I hope this works and that she did not call the county. I need more time. You know what to do."

Ben knew that he was a manic depressive. He told Vicki that he needed the weed to survive.

"I will quit this shit, as soon as I can, but right now, I need it," he always said.

When Vicki woke at six in the morning, Ben was gone. She had told the agency that she would have to take a vacation day, so that the inspection could take place. She sat in the cool early winter air, on the front porch, laden with thermal blankets and dogs.

With very hot coffee in hand, she awaited the critical inspector.

She heard a light knock on the front door at about eleven thirty. She answered it and showed the inspector inside, nervously.

"Hi, sorry that I am a little late, but I got held up on a job site," the inspector explained. "Now, let's look the property over. Where is the heater and the A.C. unit?"

Vicki showed him.

He passed those two elements. "Now for the plumbing."

He looked at the bathrooms first and passed them. Then, he inspected the washer and dryer and passed them.

Lastly, he looked under the sink and found the water pipe, leading to the drain in the kitchen sink was not assembled. He revealed this to her.

She told him, "It was assembled yesterday. I washed dishes yesterday evening." She thought, "It must have come apart somehow...or was pulled apart by *someone*."

The inspector noted, "If you happen to screw it together, I will forget that I ever saw it pulled apart."

She nodded her head and got on her hands and knees to put mold the pipes back together with tools. Ben never knew that Vicki was mechanically inclined. She put the parts back together, enough to pass final inspection. It was easy for her.

Then, it was time for the all-important insulation report, to make sure it was the *right grade*, as Ben always put it. The inspector found the insulation to be adequate, but *not good enough to pass.* "You need another *grade of insulation* throughout the house," he informed her.

"I don't know anything about that, or how it happened. My husband is in charge of that, and he isn't here right now," she said.

"Well, the only way that I can pass this house, is if you replace it all with the *right grade.* YOU can even do it, if you have to," he told Vicki, displaying an unprofessional, sleazy grin on his bruised, gangster-looking face. *The inspector* wrote out what insulation she needed to purchase.

That night she went to the family-owned building supply shop in Byhalia to purchase what insulation she was told she needed. The clerk advised her not to buy it, because it was not "code-effective", in other words, it would not pass code. He pointed to the insulation that she needed to pass.

She frowned and shook her head, "No sir. This is what I need," she stressed, pointing to the piece of paper that the man gave her and that the clerk was now holding, while shaking his head back and forth. "This is the *grade* that the building code inspector said I needed to get to pass my final inspection."

"Miss, I have lived and worked here for over twenty years, and I have built three houses myself, all in this county. I know every inspection officer well. This insulation is not acceptable. You will never pass with this stuff," he stressed. "By the way, it is called *R-value*, not *grade.* What is this inspector's name?" he questioned Vicki.

"He did not give me his name," she clarified.

"What's his number?" the clerk asked.

"I put it in my phone. Here it is," she said, showing it to him.

"This is not the number for building codes. You most likely have been dealing with an imposter. Here, give me your phone. I want to dial the number," and he dialed it.

A sultry female voice answered the phone. He hung up.

"Yep, you have been had. You need to report this with building codes, as well as the police," he advised.

She sighed, shrugging her shoulders. "Yes, I have been had alright," Vicki mumbled, as she left the shop.

Now, she knew that Ben was behind this. This would have cost her plenty of time and money in fines, if built and sold, without a "real" final inspection.

"Why is he doing this to me?" she screamed, hitting the steering wheel in disgust, as she cruised over the highway hills.

SIXTEEN

Cousin to the Rescue

Ben came back again, more revived and happy, yet tired and sad. She was used to this state of being, with the mental condition of his that came and went, and seemingly with ease.

He sheepishly said hello to Victoria and put all of his tools in their proper places, which he seldom did. She knew he was trying to butter her up, for some reason, so she played the game to see what was in store for her.

Ben made Vicki his famous pineapple spaghetti dish, complete with baked garlic bread and Caesar salad. Everything he made from scratch and was very tasty.

"Yes," she said to herself. "He definitely wants something. Let's see what it is now."

After dinner, the truth came out. While taking his dish to the sink, he mentioned to Vicki that he had found a new construction job, as a supervisor. He mentioned that he was excited, but stressed, so he needed some cash to get some "real good stuff, only to ease his anxiety".

Vicki laughed, threw her hands up in the air and sarcastically said, "Sure. Take me too, and my house."

"Honey, please," he groaned, stroking her neck. "Hey, whatever happened with the inspection? Did they come?"

"Sure did," she answered.

"It didn't pass, did it?" Ben smugly asked.

"Almost, just one thing's wrong now. I have a little time to take care of it," she spoke with newfound authority. "Hey, did you know about the insulation not meeting code?"

"Oh, no. It must have been one of the boys I hired. That's tough. It will take a lot of time to change that out," he lied.

"Well, there are to be no more of your boys on this property," she commanded.

"I decided to call my cousin when I was eating your meal. He will fix it. I'm sure."

"You are not to ever call him to do my job around here. Plus, he is expensive and busy, I hear. Don't you ever!" and he took a glass from the kitchen counter and smashed it on the newly-installed tiles on the floor, breaking many.

Victoria was in shock. She put her hands on her head and knelt down on the ground. She knew from this point on that in order to finish the house, sell it, and move on, she had to act dumb and pay his price, whatever it may be, for her own safety and security, and that of the dogs as well. She didn't know what he was thinking.

"Then, I'll do the job myself," she lied to him, just to get him to stop his maniacal behavior.

"Yeah, right," Ben smirked, as he walked over to the home phone, kicking her yelping dogs and called one of his dealer friends to buy a bag on credit.

"You know I have it coming soon man...okay, be there in a few," she heard him say to the receiver. "You come with me. We need to talk, baby."

"About what? We both know we are like salt and pepper. It just doesn't work."

"Let's go, just up the highway."

"Fine," she said, fearing her life, but her gut told her she had to go.

Once rolling on the pavement in her car, Ben put his arm around his wife, leaned over to kiss her and handed her a check for two hundred and fifty dollars.

"This is for you, from one of my paintings that my grandmother bought from me today. She is going to give it to her sister for her birthday. Her sister loves impressionism, so I guess she just really wanted to help us," he admitted to Vicki.

"That is so sweet that she did that. I appreciate anything now."

"Well, I thought you could loan me a hundred from that check, and you still have one hundred and fifty left, right?"

"It's not as sweet a deal as I thought. When will you pay me back? Do you really have a 'real' job, and when will you get paid?"

"I start tomorrow, for real. It should be close to what you make each week, and they pay out every two weeks. I will be working all the time with these people. They are making so much money and are super busy."

"I will do it this last time, but Ben, you have to get help. You know how you get with your 'withdrawal' bouts and how much money you spend each

week. We need this money to live, not to get high....
please, please do this for me, and our marriage."

"You know I will, and thanks," He muttered,
as he sharply turned into the dealer's dirt drive,
where Ben hopped out. Vicki spied a small country
house, situated in the middle of a forest on top
of a slanted hill. She stayed in the car for what
seemed over twenty minutes. Ben came back to
the car beaming with delight, pointing to a muddy
old clunker to her right.

"He gave it to me."

"Yeah, and what did you have to do for it?"

"Not much, I just need a car. You know work starts
tomorrow in Memphis. I've got to be there at seven
sharp. Are you proud, toots?" he assuredly asked
her.

"I just don't want you to deal in drugs. I hate it."

"I know, and it will soon be over. I promise," and
he got into his new, old car and peeled out of the
drive, leading the way back to the house.

How many times had he said that to her. She
couldn't even count how many.

She didn't want to think anymore. She was tired
and had to work in the morning, and so did Ben,
supposedly. She never knew if he were telling the

truth or not. It seemed now that their whole marriage had been a huge lie.

At dawn, the alarm clock went off. Both scampered out of bed, quickly got showered and dressed and hit the road for their respective jobs. Vicki knew that she had several clients to see about respective holiday trips. It would be hard work to try to piece a decent-priced holiday trip for these families, all at the last minute, but she suddenly felt invigorated in the cool, dry air.

Her confidence level this morning was rather high, and she did not know why. Maybe because Ben was going to a job that was not associated with the house, or maybe because she had the feeling he was really going to try to become drug-free. Maybe his new job would help him out, too. Most of all, however, she finally felt a glimmer of hope, as far as their finances were concerned.

If it were true that he was to bring home as much as she were, and that was only probable, not certain, then they would be able to pay off all of their house bills, all of the credit used, as well as the loans against the two CD's at the bank. This was the fourth job Ben had held since she had met him, in between episodes of home building, so Vicki was not sure how it would ultimately work out for him, *and her*.

"Maybe God is working overtime for us," she thought, as she drove along the country road, toward civilization. "Hopefully, this job will work out for the both of us."

Vicki got to work early and stayed late, trying to piece together two trips during Labor Day weekend. There were no seats left, except for Y class, or full coach fare. These were refundable, but since it was only six and seven days until their desired departure dates, this fare was not important. Each family said that they were expected at their desired destinations.

After lunch, she reserved and ticketed "consolidator" passage for round-trip travel to Glasgow, Scotland for the large family. In Memphis, many families were of Scottish-Irish blood. This family was one of these. The other family of three wanted a direct flight to and from Santa Fe. It seemed that a member of their extended family had reserved rooms for everyone in Taos, New Mexico for the holiday weekend. It was a little too late, Vicki had told the family, but still not impossible.

At the last minute, before she left the vacant office for the evening, four K class tickets lit up on the airline computer she was using in the back office. She called the family who lived in the neighborhood and excitedly booked the three, entering credit card information in the system. Seats were going to be tricky, however, she told them when they entered the building. They had to be assigned when they checked-in at the counter.

"At least we got the cheaper seats and didn't have to change planes," she affirmed to the family, "and you don't have to take your daughter out of school early to make the flight," she smiled.

Their eight-year old daughter curled up her face and made a funny expression.

She printed the tickets, and all three left the agency.

In the car, she dialed her cousin's cell to ask him about the tiles. She thought about asking him if he had time to piece together the kitchen cabinets they had had sitting in boxes for two months, in the middle of the kitchen.

"I hope I can afford this now. It would really feel like a *home* if the full kitchen were installed," she thought to herself.

Even though the house was not finished all the way, it was as far as code issues were concerned for the electrical, plumbing and foundation-support works. The comfort issues of the abode were definitely unresolved, and she wanted to put an end to this. This included having the proper insulation.

The phone rang off the hook, until she finally answered it. Her cousin was outside on a job. He worked day and night and was even more of a workaholic than she was. She explained the situation and how it needed to be done quickly. He agreed to come the next evening to start.

"Thank you Jay-Jay," as she affectionately called him. "I just really want to get this done, because the inspector that came out was evidently a hoax. He told me to get the wrong 'grade' of insulation. The workers already installed the right type, but he ripped a lot out. He's destroying my house, just like my husband," she yelled into the receiver.

"If I re-did the insulation for the whole house from scratch, it would have taken forever, first off trying to save money from each paycheck. Then there is the time factor. It would have never been completed. I am just glad I met that man and decided to go to a small hardware store in the county, instead of in Tennessee. No one there would have probably known the correct *R-value* to pass, as I have heard it called."

After drinking a glass of water to calm her nerves, she advised her cousin, "All you need to do is replace the torn-out pieces of insulation, and it should pass final. The cabinets are just an extra. At least there is a stove and oven, and a partial counter with some storage, otherwise, I don't know what I would have done with myself all these weeks. *I need this Jay.* Thanks again. I'll see you tomorrow evening."

"Sure thing, *cuz*," he chuckled. "Oh, and what company did you use for the drywall?"

"We don't have it yet," she stated. "I was counting on Ben to do it, or get the guys to do it."

"You cannot pass a final without it. You better find a drywall place that is licensed in your county, and fast. It's hard to find reputable ones down there. I don't know of one myself," he advised her.

"You know, I am almost broke from this. Right now, we are two months behind on completion. The only bank that would have given us a loan to pay back and continue building advised me that if it took more than six months to build, it would be virtually impossible to qualify for a loan, due to the amount that has been charged on my credit cards.

I'm screwed, just screwed," she moaned to her cousin. "Why did the inspector say he would approve the final without dry wall? He really is a fake! That's what the guy at the building supply shop in Byhalia thought. I didn't believe him, but now…Oh, I have no idea what's going on," she rambled on.

"I think I do. Why don't you call county building codes and ask to speak to that inspector? I think you will be surprised. See you tomorrow," he ended the unfortunate call.

After the news of Ben's job acquisition, the couple had been getting along better than ever, at least for a day or so. It confused her, like always, why she uncontrollably fell back in love with her husband. While he was addictive, so was she.

Ben's job proved legitimate, and Ben acted like a true husband for a short while, until the newness had worn off and he became bored with routine.

"Where are my jeans? Can't you wash more and be a real wife to me?" he asked.

"I would love to be a real wife to you, so maybe I should quit my job, just so I can take care of you, right?" she asked her husband.

"Don't be stupid. I couldn't take care of you, too. I can barely take care of me," he exclaimed.

Finally, she had had enough and courageously revealed to Ben the truth about what she found out about the final inspection and inspector in sly, clever fashion.

"Sit down, now," she ordered to Ben.

"What do you want?" he curiously asked her.

"I want you to call the county building code office, you know, to set up a time for the **real final inspection** by the county. I have the number right here," and she gave it to him. I have fixed the two problems myself, so we should be good to go," she lied, awaiting a reaction, and got a look of surprise.

"YOU DID IT ALL BY YOURSELF…THE ENTIRE HOUSE?" he barked in amazement, with horrified disbelief written all over his unshaven face, that she would be able to rectify his self-made building dilemmas so quickly, and all by herself. It didn't add up to him. He paced back and forth in the living room, until he saw flashing blue lights pull into their gravel driveway.

"Oh, shit. Now what?" he yelled.

Soon, there was a tap on their front door. Ben opened it and was greeted by an unhappy, large police officer.

"I need to talk with Victoria Morris," he asserted.

She came from around the corner, and he motioned for her to follow him outside. He walked down the steps and over to his car. "Come in. I would like to talk in private."

The policeman said that the clerk at the hardware shop, where he was patrolling, thought there was a situation that law enforcement should be aware of. There might be a building code imposter in the area.

"The clerk said he looked in the county records and found a property in building status, not yet complete, in the area that you had mentioned to Bob where you were building. He handed me this address." The policeman then asked Vicki for a description of the imposter and a possible motive for him wanting to do something like this.

Frightened, Vicki now let go and expounded on her domestic situation, with her husband and her finances, and his seeming desire to never get the house finalized. Vicki informed the policeman that the inspector had found two issues, one with the kitchen drain connection, and the other with the insulation throughout the house. He got out of his car with his phone, and said he would be right back.

When he returned, he informed Vicki that the house is nowhere near completion.

"And there has to be drywall, covering the insulation," he informed her.

"I know. My cousin already told me that," she replied to the policeman.

Changing the subject, he asked her directly, "Has your husband ever been in trouble with the law before?" he asked Vicki.

Astounded with that question she replied, "Oh my God, no."

"Well, let me ask you this. Has he ever laid a hand on you?" asked the officer.

"Not really," she blatantly lied. She wanted to keep the past to herself.

"What does *not really* mean? Has he ever hit you when he was angry?"

"He has, but it did not hurt much. I got banged up, but nothing broken," she cried.

The officer continued, "I did some research on him and found that he does have a record."

"What?" she exclaimed.

"It seems that the father of a seventeen year old girl turned him in. They settled out of court, however."

"What happened?" she asked him, dropping her head down.

"The girl told her father that he tried to sexually assault her on the beach. The only snag was that she was not yet an adult, and Ben said that she had lied about her age. She denied this. Ben said the girl was lying. The father wanted to take the matter to a higher court and finally, Ben's grandparents settled the matter with money, to keep it out of any court. He seems like a troubled man. This type is possessive, controlling and can be quite violent at times."

He pulled out a briefcase and grudgingly opened it. He pulled out several horrific photos of domestic abuse in the county, some were dead, others scarred and maimed for life.

"Shut it, please!" she shouted.

"I am sorry ma'am. I just wanted you to be aware of what you are up against. Please be careful. Call us if you need us," he humbly spoke.

"Thank you. I will," she spoke softly, as she got out of the vehicle to walk up to the front door. She didn't know what she would say to Ben.

She walked inside the foyer, heard nothing, so she proceeded to walk through the living room into their bedroom. Ben was not there. She ran upstairs, and no one. Vicki peered through the upstairs window to see if Ben's newly acquired car was still parked in back. It was there.

"Where could he be? He must be in someone's house on this street. Was it possible he was sleeping with someone in the neighborhood?" she thought, as she again peered out the upstairs window to look out into the night. This time, however, she turned the lights off.

That was when she saw them. Vicki saw figures in the night air walking around the house and her vehicle. These hooded pedestrians tried to get inside the car, but it was locked. She ran downstairs, turned off the rest of the lights, grabbed a knife and opened the front door, ready for a fight. No one was there.

Fuming mad, she poured a glass of Merlot for herself, drank a few sips and went to bed, so ready for a tranquil weekend. She had to work from nine until one that Saturday.

All were working at their stations, since it was so close to a holiday weekend. All agents were super busy with leisure and corporate travel. Vicki took a coffee break and spied a flier on somebody's desk that advertised a FAM trip to St. Kitts. FAM trips, or familiarization trips, were offered to all agencies as a promotional, selling tool, at rates of almost nothing. She wrote down the web address to book the trip. The travel agency gave her one week paid leave for FAM trips.

She booked the trip online at her desk for only seventy-five dollars per person double occupancy, for round-trip air and transfers, and four nights at an all-inclusive hotel. She lived to travel and traveled to live. Her mindset had now totally changed. She was excited to tell Ben about the trip she found, if she could ever find him.

She wanted to disregard what the officer told her the night before in his car. She wanted to forget about the hooded figures scoping her house and her car.

"They were probably just teens, getting into trouble. They never tried to get into the house, through any door, and we have a lot," she told the co-worker who sat beside her.

"Yes, but you also have a lot of big dogs too," her co-worker reminded Vicki.

After work, she picked up steaks for dinner. When she pulled in the drive, she noticed Ben playing with the dogs out back.

"Hi, honey," he said. "What did the cop say last night to you? Sorry I left, but *me* and cops don't get along, not with the bags of bud I have upstairs. I stayed with Dave next door."

She knew he was telling the truth, so she decided to tell him what the officer said about the assault on the beach. Ben admitted that he was charged, but denied the allegation, saying that she lied to him about her age. Ben added that the girl came onto *him*.

"I think her parents just wanted money. They planned the whole thing," he declared to his wife.

"That is rough," she solemnly said, "but…uh…he showed me all kinds of gruesome photos of women beat by their husbands and boyfriends.

After the policeman left, and I went inside, I saw hooded figures walking around the property. One even tried to open my car door, like they were looking for something inside. Do you think these were just kids from the neighborhood?"

"Probably. Hey, just let me know if it happens again, okay?" Ben stressed.

She paused, then continued. "I have a surprise for us," Vicki said, as she took out vouchers.

"What are those?" Ben asked.

"We are going to St. Kitts for four nights, over Labor Day."

"That sounds great, but I just started *another* job."

"Well, just let *another* foreman handle your houses for two days," she replied in disgust. "It will only be Friday and Monday that you will have to take off. Tell them that you already had this planned."

"Okay, screw this job, if they don't like it," he laughed.

They both went out back to start their usual campfire, with logs in hand.

SEVENTEEN

Trip from Hell

And so, they spent a quiet end of summer. Afterward, they both went back to their work schedules, which were both not that busy, since the summer was gone. So she had time during her work day to look up dry wall companies and get prices. Vicki called six companies that had good ratings from customers. They were all extremely expensive. In different phrases and wordings, they all said, however, that their services were worth the price they charge.

Vicki saw one company on the fourth internet page that was located in the next Mississippi county over from theirs. The blog said that their building specialists all have the perfect skills, supply the perfect materials and clients are perfectly happy with the service this business provides.

She immediately dialed the number listed and got a recording. Vicki left her name and number, and waited. She was searching for cheaper prices, with quality work.

Vicki went down the hall into the lobby of the office building and walked into a sandwich shop to sit at the counter and get a bite to eat. At that moment, her phone rang. It was the dry wall company.

She quickly asked the owner to give her an estimate on the square footage in her house. The price that he stated was far less than the other six had given her.

Plus, he was a lot nicer and less impatient than the others. She asked him to book a date for her when they could get started.

"It will have to be after we get back in town," she told him, "say, in about two weeks?"

"We aren't available for a complete home job for three. Is that okay? If it is, I will schedule it for then, at 8am on Tuesday morning. Everybody and all pets need to be off the premises for five days, while we do the work," the business owner informed her.

"Sure, I understand. No problem, sir. Do you take credit cards or cash?" she asked.

"We do take credit cards, with a one and a half percent interest fee added, but we prefer cash," the owner verified.

"It will have to be credit," she said.

"Alright then. See you soon," he replied.

And so the couple went on their merry, merry way to the Caribbean, ready to have a little bit of sun, fun and relaxation, before the final building stages were to begin. Ben knew that she was catching on to the building process and that he couldn't demand a whole lot more from her, with the way things were going. He knew she had taken out a small whole life insurance policy on herself, with Ben as the sole beneficiary. He was ready, if the opportunity presented itself.

The plane landed. They retrieved their luggage and hopped into their hotel bus. It wasn't long before they arrived at their hotel. From the moment they checked in, Vicki knew it didn't feel right. She, all of a sudden, did not want to be there, or with Ben.

They threw their bags in the rather bare hotel room and strolled out to find the beach bar. They sat on two bar stools in the middle of the empty bar.

Soon after, however, the open-aired bar filled-up, with scantily-dressed young babes and handsome, well-built studs, all engrossed in meaningless conversations. It made her want to gag when her own husband started conversing to them in the same tone. He ordered her one *fru fru* drink after another. These Singapore Slings only had not a full shot of alcohol in each, as she saw when they made each one for her. This was the only reason she kept on drinking. She felt fine, other than she had to take periodic ladies room breaks.

A little over an hour later, she returned from the restroom only to find her beloved carrying on with another. She appeared to be a jet black haired tramp who had her hands all over him, and his all over her. Her bathing suit top revealed her protruding nipple, as it was falling off one of her breasts. She was in a terribly drunken state. He was not. He had only gotten started.

All of a sudden, Vicki felt very weak and weary, and rather incoherent.

"Wow," she said to Ben. She couldn't even be a little mad at him. She felt like she was about to pass out.

After that episode, she couldn't remember anything until she woke up early that night. She was in her hotel room with the managers of the hotel standing around the bed. She was still out of it. They asked her questions about herself and her husband, then they left the room.

Vicki slept until the early morning sun began to shine through their sliding glass door. She felt more normal, yet her memory was not good. Her husband was not there. The phone rang and the hotel workers informed her that her husband had been placed in another room, and that he had requested this for his security.

"Security?" she shouted into the receiver. "I need to see him, and right now. He must have drugged me, or one of his cronies, last night."

"That I do not know. I will ask our manager if your husband can come to see you for a few minutes," he said, and slammed down the phone.

A few minutes passed, then a knock sounded on the door. It was Ben, escorted by the manager. The manager glared Vicki's way, then left the room.

"What the hell happened?" she asked.

"Well, you just changed, after your third drink. You passed out. We put you on a beach chair. You woke up and started yelling at me and trying to hit me.

That was when management was called. They put you in the room and me in another, for both our protection."

"I didn't *just change*. I lived with a drinker for years, and sometimes I even drank as much as he did. We just sang and had fun. This has *never* happened to me before, especially not with three mild

Singapore Slings. I know what you wanted. You wanted to put a drug in my drink, or drinks, so that you could go out and score on the beach," she blurted out.

"I did not. I have always loved you so much. Do you think I want to be with these disgusting women? No way. I'd rather be by myself. I put nothing in your drinks. You just had too many, I guess. You can't hold them like you used to, maybe," Ben suggested.

"We just got here, and already, I am so embarrassed," she told him. "I am so hungry. I didn't eat last night. I'm going to breakfast," she told him.

He followed her to the restaurant, where they barely spoke. She left the restaurant, after eating three scrambled eggs, bacon, and a waffle, with juice. She felt stronger suddenly.

He followed her to their hotel room and asked, "Do you mind if I stay here with you tonight?"

"Nope," she spoke, trying to change her mood, and she got ready for her tour around the island. Ben stayed in the room.

When she returned, hours later, he wanted to make love. Vicki refused. Ben lit up a joint which he said he bought on the beach last night. Then he slammed down a couple of beers. He sat outside, watching the view, the beautiful beach, and the beautiful bodies, until he had had his fill. He came inside and raped her, holding her mouth shut the entire time, so she couldn't scream.

Vicki got out of the bed, demoralized, and took a shower. Ben jumped in to quickly clean himself, then grabbed a towel from the rack, shaved and splashed on cologne, before putting on his skin-tight short-sleeved shirt and skin-tight black jeans and leopard boots. He was ready for the night.

She put on a rather matronly green dress, with flats, and a headband around her head, as he looked at her approvingly and did not utter a sound. She knew this is how he liked her to dress, like a "good girl". If she dressed any other way, it would start a fight, for sure. She did not want that tonight. He liked to look at her, in a plain way, knowing that she was his and nobody else would desire her. He did, however, fantasize about all of the others, those who were provocatively dressed.

Ben had never wanted his women to dress like that, like his mother used to, when she left him to go out drinking with men at bars.

At nine years old, he would have to go looking for her in each neighborhood bar and pull her out when he found her. These episodes damaged him for life. That was why he wanted a "Plain Jane" by his side, while he gazed every night through windows at single women. Many of these he would see, as he waited in club parking lots, waiting to follow them home. Ben was a twisted soul.

Later that night, after dinner, they went back to their room. Vicki interrogated him about another girl, who she had seen him flirting with at the bar, before dinner.

Ben was either wasted on drinks, or high on drugs, or both. He opened their mini-refrigerator, took out a beer bottle and struck it over his victim's head, then passed out himself.

Vicki fell to the tiled floor, but managed to pick herself up, after several minutes. She then was able to walk to the hotel clinic. She had seen the arrows pointing to it from outside of their room, so she knew where to go. They examined her forehead and skull and administered antibiotics and antiseptics to the abrasions. They asked her what had happened.

She told them the truth. The nurses asked Vicki if she wanted to press charges. They advised her that if she did, he would probably never be released. Vicki replied, "No."

The two left the island together a day and a half later. Vicki had not seen much of Ben, and they had not slept together. Victoria didn't know where he had been, nor had she cared. She only wanted to get home and back to work. She couldn't believe how relaxing her job was, compared to this vacation.

When she arrived at the agency the following day, ready to work, she was met with nonchalant workers. They had always been cheerful and vocal when Vicki came in every morning. This morning, however, they were different. They seemed to almost be looking down their noses at Vicki. She continued doing her work that morning, as diligently as possible, until she got a call from the personnel office in the back. The head officer was requesting to see her, now. She ran back.

The personnel chief asked Vicki to sit down, then told her that he received a call on Saturday from the hotel manager saying that Vicki was not coherent during the FAM trip. "He said that you were having some trouble, and that you acted like you were on drugs the entire time. What have you to say?"

"What I have to say," Vicki told him, "is that I was drugged, probably by my husband, so he could have fun while I was asleep, and that is all I was doing. He even busted a beer bottle over my head. The clinic asked me if I wanted to press charges. I said no. They said if I did he would be there forever, so I said, no. I can't remember anything else. I am sorry, but some-body did this to me. I don't do drugs and have never done anything like that. I only drink, occasionally, which is what I did, a few fancy, weak drinks, not for getting intoxicated on. Now, may I leave?"

"You may," he clarified. "But this has been a very embarrassing situation for our travel agency that we are not used to," and he closed the door behind me after I left.

It was a struggle for Vicki to keep this job and the other two, teaching a language class in the morning twice a week, and tutoring three nights a week.

She was having a hard time keeping her head together now.

Her husband had been acting like a stranger to her, and he had been moving from one job to another, never satisfied. Needless to say, not much work got done on the home.

One week later, while driving to the school to teach her French class, she heard the panic on the radio that the twin towers in New York had been hit by a plane, then another, which then pointed to terrorism.

At the travel agency later that morning, she arrived there to find the business virtually shut down. She went into the break room to join everyone, who was sitting on the couch, the chairs, and the floor, crying, watching the television set screen, amazed. They all hugged.

One month came and went with no new clients, even the existing corporate accounts were not traveling much. The United States was in a virtual lock-down.

Vicki was asked to see the personnel manager for the last time, in his office. He gave her a discharge paper, which she signed and gave him a carbon copy, then told her they hate to see her go, but they are downsizing because of this incident.

"You are entitled to unemployment with our company," he reassured her.

She left the company with a puzzled look on her face. She asked herself if this was actually due to this act of terror, or was it really because of the incident in St. Kitts that she had earlier dismissed.

Driving had always proved good for her mind and soul, and so when she arrived at her half-built home, she knew. She knew that she had to go back to graduate school again, so she enrolled for the spring semester.

EIGHTEEN

ARSON

The drywall company started working on their scheduled start date. There was a crew of four, two tomboyish women, a young man, and the middle-aged owner. They all were extremely nice and very neat. Vicki thought that she finally had a good company doing work at her house. She felt almost as confident with this company as she did with her cousin's expertise of blowing-in insulation.

"This is a first," she specified to the owner.

Ben and Victoria lived in a hotel room that had kitchen facilities included for over one week. She cooked their favorite, spaghetti with pineapple chunks, almost every night. They went shopping at the local market every day. This seemed to bring a sense of softness to their already hardened marriage.

When the drywall was finished, they scoped it, and both decided it looked immaculate. Vicki gave him an extra hundred for the job.

"This definitely was the most professional company that either of us has hired the entire time," she noted to Ben.

"I think so, too," he replied with dismay. Everything is running too smoothly and quickly, he thought to himself. "She is less dumb than I thought." He silently hit the new drywall with his fist to get out some of his anger.

Victoria loved going to school again. During her first month as a re-admitted grad student, she learned the ropes again, did a lot of work, and made A's. She was already getting to be a well-respected scholar in education academics and was offered a job, teaching Spanish and Reading to middle school students. It was in a suburb of Memphis that used to be nice and family-oriented, but now it was hardened and drug-oriented. She took the opening, anyway.

Since she was a graduate student at the university, she was eligible to teach without a certificate. She taught on a permit. The pay was better than what she made before, with much better benefits included.

The students in the Spanish one and two classes were very smart and energetic. The reading students, on the other hand, were not. Some of them could not read or write at all. Victoria was devastated with this harsh discovery.

When she went to her mail box for the first time, she was greeted with an unwelcoming phrase.

"Good luck. You're going to need it," the female voice stated.

When Vicki turned, she saw a middle-aged African-American woman standing there, with mail in hand, shaking her head and saying, "It's a war zone here," and she walked out of the mail room.

Victoria was perplexed.

For the next two weeks, she was surprised that during lunchtime, a group of five girls, from different ethnic backgrounds, would always want to sit at her desk and eat with her, out in her trailer. Vicki had never been concerned about being put out in a trailer alone, until shortly after these lunch events started.

One day, one of these girls shouted loudly, "What's the matter, Mrs. Morris?

Are you scared of us?"

At the end of that same day, she assigned some homework in her last period reading class. A riot broke out, because of this, and a tall bully threw a small Mexican rock, which was displayed on her desk, at her left eye. It skimmed the edge of her eye, barely hitting the skin. All of the students ran out of the trailer.

The assistant principal called Vicki into her office to ask her how she wanted to proceed with the assault.

Vicki told her not to press charges.

The African-American assistant principal simply shook her head and said, "Okay."

The student was a seventeen year old eighth grader, who had not been able to get a grasp on Math, Reading, or English. The school sent him to a juvenile facility for four days for conducting this episode. After that, she never saw him again.

For one week after that everything was calm, until one day, when again assigning homework in reading class, and while walking down the aisles, looking at students' work, she was stabbed. She was stabbed not with a knife, but with a large, thick, sharp pencil, by an extremely large and weighty eighth-grade boy. It was the worst pain she had ever felt.

She could not let her emotion show, however. She knew she would have paid the price, with laughter and their new-found feeling of supremacy. Just then, the bell rang.   Class was dismissed.

She managed to hobble down to the main building where there was to be a meeting, trying to find out who the teacher was, who was grading tests unfairly. Vicki had no time for this now, and she told them that.

"I'm in such pain. I have to see my doctor, now," and she got up from the conference table.

The principal who had agreed to hire her and who had wanted to eventually give her tenure, was now at a loss for words. When able to speak, he told Vicki and everyone else that they could not leave the room until he found out who this teacher was.

At that moment, all of the teachers stood up from their chairs to stand by Vicki. They told the principal that if he did not let Victoria leave for the doctor, they would all leave too. He agreed, and she hurried to the car with assistance.

The doctor did not remove the piece of led, lodged in the upper thigh of Vicki's.

He said it might become infected, if he did that. He gave her antibiotics and pain killers to take for one week.

Vicki never returned to finish out the year. She called the board of education and advised them of her decision.

"I would never feel safe working there again," she informed them.

The head of the placement division said that he understood, and that she would be paid for one additional month.

Vicki went to see two lawyers the next morning. Both informed her that they would not be able to take her case, because the perpetrators had no money, and that the school system was owned by the government. She was upset at this scam of unjustness but had no time or resources to tackle the problem, so she gave the idea up and headed home.

Here, she found Ben working at his computer, trying to find a new place of employment, like always. He was not happy working in a routine. He always got bored and rebellious, walking off the job. She was now used to how he was.

Downstairs, she called a lawyer, located in the head city of the county, whom she had met, only once in a grocery store in the county seat. She joked to him and the cashier about her "misguided" husband, while they were waiting in line. He slipped her a card and asked her to call.

He was a "cowboy" lawyer, who was a little older and very gruff. She felt like he could demand anything from anyone and get the job done. She told him that she had to do some thinking though, before actually hiring him, and setting a divorce in motion.

"Of course," he advised Vicki. "I am always here. If you need me."

Vicki went upstairs to unwind and watch some television, in the lounge area. Ben came in the room afterward. He massaged her neck. She turned on the television with the remote. He continued massaging her neck, then began kissing her all over, until they heard a news segment on a criminal wanted series.

The announcer said that a reward was available for any information given on an arsonist. He showed a picture and gave the arsonist's name.

Ben and Vicki starred at each other in horror.

It was the face and the name of the owner of their drywall company, the worker who had been so professional and amiable. The best they had hired, so far.

"How ironic," they both said to one another.

Ben called the authorities to tell them of what had transpired with the company.

He gave them the drywall company's address and phone number, hoping for a reward for retrieval of the arsonist. When the authorities arrived to arrest the criminal, he was gone. The drywall company was no longer.

NINETEEN

The lock-ups

Vicki was a happy unemployed soul now. Happy, because she felt as though she needed a break, a long break, through the entire spring and summer, at least. Ben was now happily employed foreman at another foundation company that was very success-ful. She felt like she wanted to *hold HIM for ransom*, as pay back.

She demanded prime steaks and Florida shrimp, which he bought, mostly due to guilt, and partly due to his maniac, depressive state, which seemed to be now at an all-time low. She enjoyed a great spring, and an even better summer, waking up late and cooking, decorating the abode, and finally, feeling like a true wife. She had a working husband now. It was fun for her, and she looked radiant. Ben could tell, but didn't like it. Vicki was getting too dependent on him.

Vicki's cousin and his helpers helped with building issues to finally bring the home up to code standards. Vicki called code headquarters, asked to speak with the supervisor to make sure that everything was legit, and finally, a final code inspection date was set. The home passed, and she proudly displayed the certificate in the front window for all doubters to see.

Now was the time to pursue the loan that she had questioned the loan officer of that company who, at that time, was willing to give her a loan to pay off the home's building expenses. The ad had stated that no one was denied. She hoped they were still in business. She called the programmed number.

The loan officer was still working there, and they both arranged a time that he could come out to take a look at the house and give a loan amount that he could offer.

"I hoped you would still be working there," she happily informed him.

"Well, it hasn't been that long, just a few months. I don't run around. I stay put," he asserted.

Vicki suddenly had a feeling of embarrassment at having said that to him, judging by his reaction.

The loan officer came at precisely the minute he said he was coming. He took a look around the house and the property and didn't have much to say, until he saw their dog, with the now full-blown mange, sitting in the corner. The dog was all he talked about or really seemed to care about from that point on.

The officer said he needed to put some numbers together in the car.

"I'll be back in a few," he assured.

After several minutes, he entered with a demeaning look on his face and sat down at the kitchen table.

"I will give you the sum you requested when we spoke. I usually give out a lesser amount, due to the decreasing property values of late. However, I have submitted my approval for the loan to our headquarters in Jackson, and it will be distributed among all of your creditors, in checks, with a small sum left for your personal use. By the way, just so you know, I only approved you for this amount because of your dog," he stated.

Obviously, being a dog lover himself, he painfully looked in Vicki's eyes and scolded her, "Your dog is in a bad way. He needs to go the vet immediately. It could be very expensive, so I approved it. I know how hard it has been to come up with money for this home, which by the way, looks pretty damn good, so all I am doing is trying to help you out."

"I really appreciate it. Thanks," she said.

"They will call you when the checks are ready for pick up in Jackson," he informed her.

"In Jackson?" she cried. "I have to drive down there? They can't send them to me?" she asked him.

"For a loan over one hundred thousand, we ask to see the client in person, you know, for security reasons," he suggested to Vicki.

"I understand," she said, thanking him profusely.

The next day, she took her sick dog to the veterinarian. The staff gasped when they saw him and said they would do everything they could to save him.

"He will need to stay here for five or six days, so that we can work on this dreaded manage. Just pray. You can call us anytime to see how he is doing," he assured her.

"I love you. I'll be back," she told her dog, as she left the office, with tears in her eyes.

Victoria managed to drive home, while drying the tears out of her eyes. Once there, she ran out of her car and unlocked the front door, ready to plop into bed and cry. She had to let out her emotions.

At that moment, the house phone rang. It was Ben. Sounding upset and stressed, he told Vicki that he was in the county lock-up for resisting arrest, after being spotted with a joint as he was driving.

Vicki couldn't believe this. First off, taking her sick dog for treatment that morning, and now her husband. He had been doing so well, not smoking or getting into addiction-frenzied states. It seemed as though his job was truly helping him beat this, so why this now?

She drove down to the jail and spoke to the policeman at the counter. He said that it had only been written up as a misdemeanor. Nothing else had been found on his person, nor in the truck. The policeman said that he had to spend that day and the next in jail and pay a fine of five hundred dollars. Vicki nodded and wrote him a check. It did not hurt so much now, knowing that she had a big, fat loan check coming her way. She could afford it now, but still despised writing it. She realized then that Ben had never grown-up. That was the problem that she faced and would continue to face, it seemed.

It brought back memories of their whirl-wind trip to Europe, where they traveled through France,

Switzerland and Italy, over Christmas and New Year's. They were gone for a total of three weeks.

Ben and Victoria, the most-striking looking couple, took this trip the year before they married. They had a massive fight in Paris that ended them up at a police station. On Christmas Eve, they became engaged in a fancy hotel overlooking the Matterhorn in Zermott, Switzerland. This was how their crazy relationship had always been, seriously up some of the time, but seriously down most of the time.

On Christmas Day, they took a high-speed train through the highest points of the Alps, on the way to Geneva, where they stayed for several nights. Then, they were onto Italy to see Venice, Rome, Florence, and Palermo, Sicily.

They had a quiet time in Venice, Florence and Palermo. Rome, however, was another story.

After sitting at the Vatican, sipping straight Vodka, Vicki left Ben to go to a nearby restroom, located in a trailer on the sidewalk. When she exited the trailer, she looked around, and found Ben to be nowhere in sight.

Feeling drunker and sicker every second, like something has been put in her vodka, she looked for him, but couldn't find him. She didn't know where she was or where she was going, but she kept on through blustery New Year's Eve, filled with people celebrating, with no taxis or buses stopping. They were all filled. She kept on walking, and walking.

Then, she realized a man was following her and speaking German. She reached for the small empty purse that she had just bought and realized it was not around her shoulder. By now, she felt like she was waking up, and that she had been in a drug state prior.

Then she felt her coat. It was wet. She did not know what evil transpired during her walk, but she thought that this foreign man, who was speaking to someone the entire time on the phone, was behind it all. Maybe he just wanted to steal a purse and that was that.

"When he finds out that there is nothing in the thing, I wonder what he will do," she asked herself. "I have to run, get in amongst the crowd, and find my way through this city, back to the hotel."

When she finally saw a familiar landmark, she knew to turn left at the bend. She walked up the block, like a cripple, after walking for almost ten miles from Vatican City to near the outskirts of Rome. She now felt safe and that she owed her safety to a higher being.

Ben was angry, upon seeing her at the hotel's door-way. The staff said he was not on the reservation, so they could not let him into the room. He had slept on the floor he said, and he was fuming. Vicki was fuming also, but she was so tired, drugged and con-fused that she didn't show it. They went to the room to sleep, and he threw her into the wall. She didn't feel it, though.

The next morning she told him what had hap-pened, and he pulled her close to him and told her he loved her. They both cried.

After Rome, they took the train to Florence where they uneventfully stayed for three nights. Then they went on to Palermo, again for a rather uneventful stay.

The couple flew to Amsterdam from there. They had an eventful stay there, for the first time since Rome. Ben bought weed down below in one of the venues. Vicki had never had any before, and this was supposedly high dollar. He negotiated and got the price down, by buying a larger quantity. This time, the money had been his.

Ben knew they were going to Amsterdam at the end of their trip to stay for three nights, before tak-ing their international flight home. He saved a wad of cash for his treat. He told her he got this money from his dad, who lives in Houston, and who had never met in his entire life.

"My father sends me this once a year, before Christmas," he said, while waiting for his merchandise to be packaged properly in plastic. "I guess this is the least he can do for me. He never did one dang thing for me and mom, not one dang thing," he told her grimacing, before ordering a shot of vodka to throw down his parched throat.

They both got high and walked down the streets of downtown Amsterdam, hitting each museum that they saw along the way.

"This is so fun!" uttered Vicki. She had never had a feeling like this one.

"See, I knew you would like it," exclaimed Ben. "I'm going take some of this back home with us. We'll have a kick-ass time with it, you know."

"Hey, you better not. That is too dangerous," she advised.

"It's not illegal here, so it's okay. Besides, I'm not going to show it to the cops. I will hide it still," Ben said. "Plus, I'm not bringing much in."

They left for the airport the next late morning. There had been a few drizzles earlier, but now it seemed to have stopped, and the sun was coming out.

They called a taxi for Schiphol airport. Once checked-in, Ben felt a sense of urgency to get rid of his illegal stash. He dismissed this fear later. He thought he was being weak and scared. He would take this small amount into the states and, they would not even care. They probably won't even know.

Ben had waded up his weed into gum balls that he thought no one would ever see.

When the plane touched down in Atlanta. They approached the escalator down to baggage claim, and that is when he saw them, the drug dogs. For a second, he panicked, but had to continue downstairs.

As soon as he got on the lower floor, he became encircled by drug dogs. Hand-cuffs were placed on Ben's hands, and he was escorted out. Vicki was told to go to a small room in the center of baggage claim, where they told her what was going on and where Ben was. A list of bail bond companies was given to her. She thanked them, then had their luggage transported to Memphis.

Later that night, after dinner and a drink at an airport restaurant bar, where she spoke with several understandings patrons, she charged money against her credit card to get enough taxi money to go to the holding facility and retrieve Ben. She had no cash left from her trip. She was told that she had to arrange for one of the companies to set bail. She only had a credit card, no cash, and found only one that would take this form of payment.

Ben was released, and they took a taxi to the Hartsfield Airport. It was about two in the morning. They securely slept, one at a time, in their seats, until their flight was called at seven.

They boarded the flight and landed in Memphis at eight in the morning.

TWENTY

THE CALL

Even though the final permit had been issued on a cold day in late March, three months ago, there were still many issues with the property. For instance, the closets needed to be finished out with rods, so that clothes could be hung from them. More importantly, the final coat of paint needed to be put over the primer, and a small concrete slab needed to be poured outside of the backdoor, so that no one sank in the mud that surrounded the house. In that part of Mississippi, it was always raining and tornado-ridden.

Her money dictated what she would be able to complete that summer. She could rely on no more income from the school system. She relied solely on Ben, which was a switch, and that was why she had never decided on a definite divorce. In the long run, he had always come up clean, she blindly smiled to herself.

Vicki hired a precise, local painter, who had been a former crystal meth addict. When he smiled, this painter displayed not one tooth because of the drug's damage to teeth. He finished the four bedrooms in record time. Vicki put the final coat on the den, living room and both eating areas. She had to wait on the tiling repair in the kitchen.

One morning, while sitting by her pond, enjoying her cup of coffee in the dense humidity in early August, her cell rang. It showed a number that she didn't recognize. She reached for the phone and fumbled, spilling her hot coffee on her wrist. She pushed in the button to answer and sounded in pain, as she answered, "Hello."

"Is this Victoria Morris?" the unfamiliar voiced asked.

"Yes, who is this?" Vicki replied.

"This is Kirk Richardson with the city school board. We have an open position for a Spanish teacher in two middle-schools, just a few miles apart, for the same pay as last semester. I was so excited that I had to call you right away. Are you interested?"

"Of course I am," Vicki stated. "Which schools are they?"

"Well, you would be teaching three classes in the morning, starting at eight-thirty, at Rose Hill Middle, then you have a two hour lunch break. After lunch, you would travel down the road to Ridgemont Middle School, where you teach two Spanish honor classes, before leaving at three."

"Well, so far, it sounds perfect," she advised him. "Do I need to sign anything, and when does school start?"

"It starts soon, in ten days, so if you could, it would be great if you could see me tomorrow morning for a formal confirmation. I will give you a packet pertaining to information on both schools, student information and course requirements for each month of the year," he formally stated, not in his prior jovial tone.

"I could be there tomorrow morning at nine, if that is alright. Where do I find your office, Mr. Richardson?" she asked.

"It is on the first floor. When you enter the building, go through the lobby and turn right, go down the narrow hallway, and my office is at the end on the left. My name is above the door. I look forward to seeing you tomorrow, Vicki," he genuinely said.

"Likewise, sir," she acknowledged, then she poured the last sip of coffee down her throat.

At sunrise the next morning, she awoke with a start. Ben was sleeping soundly beside her. He had been a good mate as of late, and she wondered how long this could or would continue. She hoped forever, but down deep inside, she knew differently.

Vicki quickly bathed. They had a whirlpool bathtub in the master bedroom, with a shower head, and no curtain to confine the water, as of yet. Their only actual shower was in the bathroom upstairs. She loved the Jacuzzi jets' feel on her tight, sore muscles every morning. It helped her get through each and every day.

She found the office of Mr. Richardson, who it turns out was the head of Human Resources. He greeted Victoria with a firm handshake and smilingly noted, "Yes, I am the person responsible for hiring and firing."

Vicki laughed and walked into his small office. He showed her to a chair, then handed her a package of documents.

"If you could sign these five papers. That is all we need. I will give you a copy of each of these. They all discuss pay, vacation time, simply all of the teaching requirements of the job. On the bottom of the first page, just read your personal information, and if it is all correct, sign below. Each of the next four pages is the same.

If you have any questions, ask me. I will be right back after I get a refill," and Kirk carried his coffee cup into the break room and hurried back.

Vicki handed him back the short stack of papers, "Here you go."

"Good luck, Victoria," he said, as he handed her a calendar for the new school year.

Excited, but still cautious, she left the building and began preparing for the soon to come school year.

The school year went by quickly and without episode. She and Ben had driven down to Jackson to pick up the checks that paid off her credit cards and one CD bank loan. The lending company said that they were not able to provide a big enough loan to pay off the second CD loan. Vicki was able to handle that well. These pay-offs helped her immensely, and she felt great. That is, until the inevitable happened.

After Christmas, upon returning to her position at her second school, she was called into the office by the principal. She had no idea what this was about. She had never missed a day, never been late, and had never a parent complaint, only praises. She was stumped.

"Whatever I am here for, I hope it is on a positive note," Vicki whispered to herself, as she slowly walked toward the secretary's desk.

"She will see you now," she said, as she led Vicki down the hall to the principal's office.

Vicki reached out her hand, as soon as she saw her body stand up. She directly asked Vicki for her folder of lessons she was going to implement for the next year. Vicki blindly shook her head.

"No one told me that this was due. I do not have it. I had no idea. I'm so sorry," Vicki said to her principal.

"That is no excuse," the principal informed her, looking down at Vicki through her reading glasses. "I need it in my office tomorrow at noon," and she stared a hole through Vicki, as she backed-up and went through the office door.

During her planning period, Vicki spoke with teachers who she saw walking toward her in the hall. These two teachers both told Vicki that it seemed as though it were a set-up.

"All of us have known about this folder for close to a year. She didn't tell you and that was her responsibility. The board wants you gone. I think the state was scared you would press the issue of what happened at your other school. That's why they offered you this job.

When I was studying law, my class discussed that when a situation occurs that warrants a law-suit, and it is forgiven. It is thus dismissed and can't be furthered. I think that was what their plan was," the older and more educated of the two declared.

"That makes sense. You really should have been a lawyer, instead of a struggling Forensics teacher," the younger English teacher added.

"I have one night to write hundreds of pages, no way, no how," Vicki verified.

"Wow. I see what you mean. It has taken me a long time to even get close to one hundred pages. I see her next week to turn my folder in. I'm *still* working on it," the older teacher revealed.

After school was dismissed, she raced home to begin her report on lessons she wanted to prepare for next year's classes. Vicki worked all evening and late into the night, preparing as many lessons, with summaries and goals as she could muster, with no advance notice. At two in the morning, she was beat and called it quits. She only had twelve pages written. She did not care. She just wanted sleep.

She overslept the next morning. She threw on a shirt and a skirt, slipped on some loafers, grabbed her report, threw her purse over her shoulder, and ran outside the door. She arrived at her first school only five minutes late, just as the students were walking into her class.

She skipped lunch and went straight to the next school for her dreaded meeting at noon. She waited for about ten minutes, until the principal called her into the office. Her secretary was at lunch.

"Is this your report?" the principal questioned, as she stared Vicki up and down.

"Yes, it is," Vicki replied meekly.

The principal read the first paragraph and slammed the stapled stack of papers on her desk and said, "You're a non-rehire." She told her to see the human resources director before the end of the month, which she did.

He held out a small check for her 401K, as well as her termination papers. Kirk added that even with a master's in education, now being classified as a non-rehire, she would never be able to land a permanent teaching position in the school system.

Vicki went through the next couple of months living in a maze, not knowing where she was going or what she was going to do. She just kept on keeping on.

One day, however, she awoke with a change of perspective. She asked herself wild-eyed, "Why do I keep going there, day in, day out, with the end in sight, with no future? I still have sixteen days of vacation time left, so why not use it. I deserve it and more importantly, they deserve it, and I will hand it back to them."

She looked on her computer and found an exciting itinerary on a luxury cruise line, leaving from Tampa. She booked the cruise by putting in her credit card information. She would have to phone in everyday and advise the machine that she was going to be absent, in order to keep getting paid. As soon as her vacation days were all used up, she would stop calling. At least, she would get some retribution, she thought. Her next week was going to be her last.

TWENTY-ONE

The Job Offer

Vicki was frantically busy getting ready for the cruise, while grading her last week of homework packets. She felt bad for not telling her students that she was leaving, but she felt that she had to do this. She had been had by the board.

Ben had been calling Vicki daily to bring him supplies that he left in the house, so that he could work on pending jobs. Everything was decent between the two of them, until one morning when Vicki delivered Ben needed supplies which were now rusted.

"I can't use these. Why did you keep these out in the rain, you slut? Now you have to go out and buy me new tools, you whore," he shouted in the parking lot.

He went inside the office for a second and came out holding a cup of coffee in his hand. His hand was shaking with anger. He opened Vicki's car and poured the cup of boiling hot coffee on her lap.

Vicki screamed, "How dare you?" and sped off in pain. Luckily he was wearing her heaviest pair of jeans, so that shielded the scorch, but it still left a huge red mark on her upper thigh. She scoped it out when she got home.

Ben did not come home until right before the cruise. She knew by now that when he got into such an angry mental state, it was best that he went away somewhere and did not come home, for her own safety and his. She knew that he needed help, serious help, and fast, but she still was excited about her cruise, with or without Ben.

Ben came running through front door, carrying a six-pack and a large pizza.

He said that he was sorry for scalding her with the hot coffee. He said he was just so stressed from work and was so excited about their upcoming cruise.

The packed their washed clothes, after finishing a delicious supreme pizza and a six-pack of ale. Ben carried their suitcases into the hallway and set them by the front door. He was so ready to leave, so ready to get away from his monotonous routine of work, which he had never liked at all.

They went to bed, never touching, or saying good night. They each went to sleep with a smile on his and her face, however. She was getting used to his maniacal behavior, which was not a good thing.

She jumped up in the middle of the night, remembering that she never called the voice machine at the board that records absences. She left a vague message saying she was ill and would be absent until further notice.

"When I feel I can teach, I will call to let you know when I will be there. Thanks," and Vicki left it like that.

In the morning, they headed to Ybor City to board the ship, which was sailing in two hours. They were given keys for their ocean view room. They hung-up and put away everything in their cases and walked quickly to get out on the outside upper deck, to find a nice spot at the bar, so that they could sit and watch, as the ship left the port.

They were voted by the guests as *the* **Most Romantic Couple** *on the ship*. No one could have ever known that they were on a shaky foundation with their marriage. They both did karaoke, work-outs, danced all night, and ate all day. It was a special time for the both of them.

The ship traveled through the Virgin Islands, ending up in San Juan. After exploring old San Juan in the morning and experiencing an authentic Puerto Rican lunch at a famous restaurant that dated back to the late eighteen hundreds, the couple caught a cab for the airport, for their one-way ticket back to Tampa. Once there, they were to stay the night, somewhere, then drive back to Mississippi in the morning.

They had boarding passes that placed them on the three-seat side, but no one else was there, as of yet. Ben placed their small bags up above them and sat down. He raised the armrest which separated his seat from the vacant one and straddled out on both.

When he got comfortable and closed his eyes, he heard a voice overhead say, "I think this is my seat."

"Okay," Ben said. "Sorry."

The voice above him said, "Hi, my name is Doug."

The voice below him said, "Hi, my name is Ben. Nice to meet you."

Doug and Ben talked the minute Doug sat and never stopped. They seemed to be friends from the start, which was rare with Ben. It usually took him years before forming a true friendship.

It turns out that Doug had recently opened a plumbing company in Tampa, where he lived, with his girlfriend. When he found out that Ben was in and had been in the construction, the electrical and most recently the foundation repair business, he raised an eyebrow.

"You know that my company needs one more plumber to round out its teams. It sounds like you know what you are talking about and could do that job," he praised Ben.

"What do you say? Does it sound good? The pay is more than decent, but you would have to move."

"Heck yeah it does, but tell me what is the pay?" Ben asked Doug.

"Call me when you get home, and we'll go over everything," he assured Ben. "Better yet, why don't you and your wife come over tonight to meet my girlfriend? Come join us for dinner. It will probably be take-out, if that's alright."

"Sure, we can make it. Give me your address, and we'll find it…still don't know where we are staying tonight," Ben revealed.

"No worries. I have a friend that manages a great Polynesian hotel up the street from my townhouse. I bet he'll even cut you a rate. I will pick you up from there at eight," Doug smiled and awaited a response from Ben.

Ben put out his hand and told Doug how much he appreciated this.

Doug smiled at Ben, then at Vicki and hailed a cab to take the couple to the hotel.

Ben and Vicki had an enjoyable Chinese dinner with the couple at their three-story luxury townhouse in West Tampa. Doug appeared to be in his early twenties and his girlfriend, Erin, a few years older. Neither one was attractive, but rather plain.

Their personalities rectified their ordinary looks, however. They were both so funny and entertaining, and Erin seemed super smart, especially regarding politics. Ben gave Doug his cell number and their address, and they parted ways.

Ben and Vicki decided to extend their overnight stay. The ended up staying at the comfortable hotel for two nights. The next day, they woke up late, went shopping at the mall and went to two renowned restaurants in the area, before leaving the next morning for their home in Mississippi.

Ben was more than excited. Every bristle of hair on his arms was standing on edge, waiting for perfection, to have the perfect life. He wanted that, and so did Vicki, with all her heart, because she still loved Ben deeply, even with all the shame and possible betrayal. She had never been able to prove this, however, so there was still hope for their marriage, she thought.

"Oh, I do hope that this job is for real and that it doesn't *back fire* on Ben. That would destroy him, *like fire*," she whispered to herself in the car.

TWENTY-TWO

THE MOVE

A s soon as Ben got to the house, he called Doug
and asked for the salary was offering. The amount
suited him royally, as Vicki could see from Ben's
expression.

"There's also commission on top of that?" Ben
wanted to make sure he heard right.

"You can make a good living, if you are willing to
work," Doug stressed.

"When are you ready for me then?" Ben questioned excitedly.

"The new team should be in place by the third
week in May," he advised, then went on. "You
should really think about driving down here during

that week. You can stay with me for a few days, while you are looking for a place. I am really excited about you joining us and hope that you like it down here like we do. Thanks again Ben," he slurred, as if drinking hard liquor in the morning.

"Anytime man," Ben answered astutely, trying to keep his good impression intact, and he started getting his large assortment of clothing, most of which was bought by Vicki. He thought it a good thing that he had three weeks to get his head together and have some fun.

The one thing that neither of them had thought too much about was the newly-built house, and of course he wasn't thinking of this right now. He had never landed a job that paid even a quarter of this salary. If he worked and produced enough, he could make close to one hundred thousand smackers per year.

With this in mind, Vicki and Ben each thought privately about keeping the house and renting it out. This way, they would be able to afford their own house in Florida, too.

"Maybe this project will have worked out for us after all," she uttered positively. "It will work out somehow. We just have to have faith. We have both put in our dues. You know Ben?"

Ben had his young dope suppliers did some handy work around the house, like putting up a railing on the walkway, a rail on the staircase, forming steps outside the two back doors, and mounting ceiling fans throughout. He paid them with Vicki's money and added a bit more for a bigger pouch of weed to last him until he left town. He was careful to cost this into the amount requested by the boys for these fix-ups.

These boys liked Vicki, even more so than Ben, who they thought was a jerk and just dealt with him for the cash. The three were on Vicki's side when Ben had an episode one morning, coming out of the shower upstairs, and he forcefully grabbed the newly-positioned wood staircase rail.

Wobbling, Ben nearly fell on his face, as the just installed railing and glued wood, came out of the wall frame. He yelled at the top of his voice and once standing erect, he ran down the stairs, trying to beat his boys for their *shitty work*, as he put it.

Upon looking into his menacing eyes coming toward all four of them who were standing by the back door, talking and laughing, she grabbed her keys and motioned for the three to follow. She started her car. The three jumped in, barely making it, as it spun almost out of control. Her husband blew out one tire with a bullet from his rifle that he was sup-posed to have sold to the pawn shop up the street, but never did.

Finally, the car got itself out of the mud that the shot-out tire sank into, and barreled off into the ho-rizon, with everyone laughing loudly. The drug boys were not Ben's real friends.

"We ain't gonna do business with him no more," said the eldest of the three.

"No, we ain't," said another.

Vicki dropped them off at a bus stop in Memphis, so that they could get home. She had met their families once before, in a not too nice part of town. Their grandparents were very nice and so were their baby sisters and brothers. They had been raised in a drug neighborhood and that was all they knew. So in a way, she admired them for being so decent.

The three, two were brothers and the other one was a neighbor, all of African-American descent, were polite and caring to her. She thought that if they turned their ways around, they could succeed at anything.

After she dropped off the boys, she never saw them again. She drove back to the property, think-ing of what she would say to her husband and how she would act, would she be mad as hell, or just a little. Should she apologize, or should he? Confusion in her mind, regarding Ben, perpetually ran rampant.

Vicki arrived home to an empty house. Benjamin had left a scathing note that he had gone early to Tampa. She hoped it would end up like this and had pretty much expected this, because of his meltdowns in the past. She came to terms with the fact that he was a very weak person, who simply could not handle anything that he did not like or agree with, especially when he didn't have his fix on, which he didn't have, not on that day.

TWENTY-THREE

THREE SUITORS

Ben called his wife from Mobile and said that he had no more money on him, after he had spent a fortune on gas, hotel and dinner. He told her he needed some help.

"Can you charge a hotel for me in Florida for a week? I'll try to earn money for my expenses, even though Doug said he holds back the first week. After I get started, it should roll like a lucky seven dice. And if I bring in customers, I get an additional commission, so I have to get some new clothes and shoes and get a haircut.

Hey, could you send me a check, a loan, to the hotel that you book. Hurry, okay, like today, after you book it. I should be there tomorrow afternoon.

Thanks toots. You're the greatest, and I'm sorry, I should have never left without saying goodbye. I just hate those leeches, unskilled, untalented leeches who just want money for doing nothing."

"Look into the mirror," Vicki inaudibly muttered to Ben.

"What? I can't hear you. Are you there?" he asked.

"Yes, but I have to go now," she told him, and cut him off.

Perplexed, he seemed to like her new attitude. It was like the chase that he never had before.

Vicki called her girlfriend, and they decided to go out for a night on the town, or a night in glittery East Memphis. They met for dinner and drinks, then continued to a club on Poplar. They were scoped by every man on the premises. The two girls were hot and dressed to kill, both with tight black minis, low cut camisole tops, and spikes. They almost looked like twins, except for the hair color. Vicki was naturally ash brown, and Nora was jet black, by way of the bottle. They talked with many a man at the bar that night, but none was "hook-up-able". That was what the two ladies thought and said to one another in private. *Then*...Vicki met John.

Big John, as he was called by his friends, was an able man, a decent-looking man, a hard-working law man, and a millionaire, and the latter really amused her and made her want to stick around, especially when she saw the house the next day. He had invited her to come over and go swimming, so he gave her his address.

When the gates opened and she viewed the two-story "Tara" mansion, she knew he was something special. The only reason this romance never evolved, however, was because of John's short-comings, of which he had plenty.

First off, he told her that he had dated a premier stripper in Tampa for many years, but had not wanted to get married. Secondly, his two children had almost been neglected by him, as he informed her, and thirdly, his second romance, after his divorce, had been with a redneck sex maniac, who he said he wanted her to meet.

"No way," Vicki stated. "I am not like that and never have been," she informed him.

She left his premises and told him she would call, but never did. He called her several times, however. She never answered.

At a grocery store one week later, she saw her father's long-time, young good-looking announcer who aired a lot of his spots. The announcer told Vicki he always had a "thing" for her, but he could never let it show. He was adored by both women and men, as he had a bi-sexual look to him. Rob had a pretty boy look to him, with spiked golden brown hair, sparkling hazel eyes and a captivating smile, complete with perfectly shaded white teeth. His body was not very manly, either. It was very slim, with mild muscle tone, and his hands displayed graceful, long fingers, like he hadn't done house or yard work a day in his life. He possessed a long torso with short legs, which stood just over Vicki's five-foot six inch frame.

He was her friend and meant nothing sexual to her at all. She especially knew this after he kissed her at the bar. They caught up on the three years in which they had not seen each other. This conversation filled with laughter and seriousness, lasted for over two hours. The most interesting aspect of this encounter, however, was hearing how he received thousands of dollar checks in the mail every day for producing "easy to make" HUD commercials.

"These people cannot afford housing, and I make it easier for them, and I also make a lot of money doing so," he bragged. He disgusted her, but yet she thoroughly enjoyed being wined and dined, as the host showed them to a nice corner table.

Robert ordered Steak Diane and scalloped potatoes, coupled with a Caesar salad, for the two of them to savor.

"Would you like to wet your whistle with a dry Martini. It will go great with dinner," Robert suavely asked her. "I'm going to order one."

"No, but I would like another glass of Cabernet," she requested.

He ordered Bananas Foster and dark roasted Peruvian coffee for both, after their scintillating dinner. He was acting like a total gentleman, of whom she had not met for what seemed like decades, since she was a child. She was beginning to slowly change her opinion of him, but not enough to change her desire to make her marriage work.

A couple of days later, Vicki "bumped-into" her first suitor at the same bar where they had met prior. His court-reporting business, and his ranch, which was located inside the city, with a two-story southern plantation home situated smack dab in the middle, had been keeping him busy, with problems attached to both. Vicki had been invited to his property to swim in his Olympic-sized pool, equipped with cabana, bar, and Jacuzzi, several times in the recent past. "Come over. I have plenty of suits," John flirtatiously commanded her.

So she did, once again, and changed into a bathing suit that he had hanging in his dressing room. The only one that seemed to be not too big and not too small for her hourglass figure. She put it on. It fit well and even enhanced her shape.

He assured her that all suits and foot-wear were completely sanitary. He had everything needed for a woman to have an unexpected day at his pool.

"He must have a lot of women," she quietly said to herself, as she looked at the array of swim suits and sandals that he had in the closet.

Once in the Jacuzzi, Big John, took off his swim trunks, and her top, and began kissing her body.

Vicki, however, was not interested in a sexual affair. She was still married, and she told him that again. Taking the comment humbly, John retrieved her top from the tiled walkway, where he had thrown it, and positioned and fastened it onto her voluptuous chest.

Big John thought that he had made some sort of headway with Vicki, when she kissed his lips sweetly and told him that she would call him.

"I hope so. We are good together," he whispered in her ear as they parted ways.

Finally, her third suitor had been a former teacher at her former school, who it turned-out, was let go, with a non-rehire status, just like Vicki's label. This third romancer was a drunk, however, and so his label was warranted.

When they worked in the same building, down the hall from one another, she would always find him staring at her, as he was perpetually passing by her room. She wondered if he ever did any teaching, so she asked him one day, "Mr. Moore, are you working, or just window shopping?"

Surprised by her direct question, he answered truthfully, "It is one of my planning periods, I have a lot, three, so I guess I am window shopping. Oh, and you can call me Paul, since we know each other now." He smiled big, and walked away.

Vicki just watched him walk down the hall, shaking her head all the while.

"Men!" she gasped, as she walked over to the water fountain. Then she rushed back to the classroom to make sure her students were doing their work. All was good.

It was as if men were being thrown on her lap at all times, as if she were on the *Dating Game* show. They asked her all kinds of personal questions and told her in different ways that they all wanted her. She only replied back with, "But you know I'm married."

They each mirrored the same reply back to hers, "Get a divorce. I'm better for you."

TWENTY-FOUR

THE FIRST TRIP

Ben had been gone for almost one month with hardly a phone call to his "beloved" wife. He sent her no checks either, which he said he was going to do. She wasn't expecting it, so it was no surprise to her. She felt a moment of peace living alone, with only her dogs. She was entertained every weekend by at least one of her three suitors. Vicki was simply having fun when she went out with each of them. She felt she deserved it, after living like a broke hermit for so long, with insults given to her daily by Ben.

Vicki was given constant compliments by her three, on dates, even on phone calls. Each one wanted to marry her. She had no intentions, however. It was strictly platonic fun for her, and she wondered how long each of them would put up with that.

She had no money left in her bank account. Her last withdrawal from the bank had been made for her husband's week-long stay in Tampa. His second call had been to tell Vicki that she had to give him more money for an additional week down there. She told him she had nothing left in her bank, and she would have to put it on her credit card.

Of course, he agreed, and said, "What would I do without you, toots? Love you."

She hated it when he called her "toots". She replied to him with, "You have to pay me back for this one. I can't pay my credit card without your help."

"Definitely," he said. "I'll call you when I can."

The next morning she picked up a paper and a coffee and biscuit from around the corner. She went home and spread out the employment section. She found one listing that really interested her. She called the travel agency/time share corporation that was based in Texas and had an office in Memphis, fairly close to where she lived.

She set up an interview with Mary for the next morning at nine, anxious to see what this company was all about.

The next morning, she left at eight, quickly dressing in black jeans and a long-sleeved polo shirt. She had no time to feed the dogs.

When she got there, she was greeted by Mary, one of the owners. The other, she found out later, was her husband, Gary. Mary was a made-up, middle-aged woman, whom Vicki could tell was once a party girl. Vicki sat in Mary's office and went the details of the job.

At the end of the interview, Mary looked Vicki straight in the eye and said, "There is something about you that I really like. We get along well. What I don't like is the way you're dressed. You should have never come to an interview dressed like this."

Caught off guard by that remark, Vicki clarified, "We just built a new house, and all my clothes are still in boxes."

"I don't care the reason, but you should not dress like you did for a job interview," Mary restated.

"I know. You're totally right," Vicki agreed.

"I want you here tomorrow at nine. We'll give you a contract for an hourly salary position, plus commissions for the time share side."

She was hired, and she felt so good she had to celebrate with a dinner downtown by herself this time.

She had to get up early the next morning. She had a good feeling.

She ended up almost running the business the moment she got there, with her travel expertise. They had a bookkeeping error which she first had to figure out. It amounted to an error of four hundred seventeen dollars from one year ago. It took Vicki about one week to come upon this error.

Once done, her career flourished. She booked one trip after another, conducted time share presentations about how to become a travel agent, for the folks that bought a time share, which many times she sold as well. Vicki was making money and doing well now, for the first time in a long time. She was happy working twelve hours a day.

After three weeks of not hearing a word from Ben, she told Mary that she was going to take the next Friday off to go down to Florida to see what Ben was doing. Mary knew that he had not phoned her for a while and was upset with what he was doing to her.

Mary said, "Fine, but I think you should leave him."

Vicki replied, "Well, you never know," then she informed Mary that she would have to come in at noon that Monday.

Victoria left after work, late on Thursday night, with her handsome, recovered dog. The veterinarian had done a great job, displaying lots of care. They both drove through the rain-filled night, through construction, small towns, and very dark, narrow, barren roads. Vicki, however, wasn't worried. She had her German Shephard with her.

They finally found a cheap motel to stay for the night. The sign said "No dogs allowed." She had other plans though. She told the East Indian woman at the desk that she was bringing her dog into the room to protect her.

"You know, I am a woman traveling alone, and he is my protection," Vicki stated.

The woman said nothing, just handed her a bill to sign and accepted the cash.

They both left at eight the next morning, driving her way through the gulf cities, down to Clearwater, where Ben ended up staying.

She called Ben and asked for the directions to his hotel once she reached Tampa. He wasn't explicit, and she ended up getting off on the wrong airport exit ramp, thus adding an hour to get to the final destination. When she finally arrived, Ben was waiting in the parking lot with roses in hand. They went out to a quiet dinner that night.

The next morning, they went to Indian Rocks Beach, had breakfast and walked along the rocky beach, hand in hand.

"I am so glad you came down to see me," he said. "Sorry I haven't called you, but I have been so busy building my business with this company. I am starting to make some money. Isn't that good?"

"Then I guess you have some to give me, for money you owe me?" she gleamed.

"Well, uh, not quite yet. They haven't paid me for the jobs yet. It takes time. Please be patient, okay," he tried to assure her.

Ben got a call at that moment. The loud voice on the other end told him that there was a client who needed emergency help with a plumbing leak, "asap". The voice gave him the address. Ben ran to his truck, with Vicki trying to keep up. He dropped Vicki off at the hotel and kept on going, up to the northern part of the bay area.

In the room Vicki had nothing to do but watch television and look at magazines on the desk. She noticed his briefcase that was open, with frayed papers coming out of it. Among those frayed papers she found an assortment of fives, tens, and twenties that added up to six hundred and twenty dollars.

"What is this? I thought you had nothing. That you were waiting. You are totally playing me, aren't you," she yelled into the empty, cold room, clutching the cash desperately. That was when she saw it, Ben's diary.

Vicki opened the diary, and not having one ounce of guilt, turned to the pages of when they first met. Here, she found pages of deceit. Every date had been teamed with girls he found, when going to the restroom. After he took Vicki home from their many dates, he had met up with these tramps, one at a time, even two at a time. Furthermore, a couple of his periodic building jobs were not for real, as he had been fired the first day for not showing up. He had been hired and fired even more than he let on to her.

"He is trash," she gritted her teeth and tore up every page of his revealing diary.

She stormed out of the hotel room with her bag, her dog, and his money. They got in the car, and headed back to her world, anxious to tell Mary what she had found, and found out.

TWENTY-FIVE

THE SECOND TRIP

Ben tried to call her cell every hour, on her ride back to northern Mississippi. She never answered one call. When Vicki arrived at her house, he called the land line and her cell over and over again, like a deranged soul. Still, she never answered one call.

Vicki worked like a leader at the agency now. After another two weeks one of the heads of the corporation who was in town asked her if she wanted to move to Texas to become one of the team players at the corporate office in Dallas.

"It would be a huge promotion, with a huge raise. We are so lucky we all found each other,

Vicki. You are the perfect fit for the company," Gary
stated, and Mary nodded.

Vicki drove home in deep thought.

She went to work early the following morning to tell
Mary of her decision.

"Mary, I really need to try to make my marriage
work one last time. That's why I have decided to
leave after work on Friday for a few days, without
pay of course. I know I've only worked her a couple of months. I need to be one hundred percent
sure before I end my relationship," Victoria strongly
spoke. "And I'm going to take my dog again."

"Agreed. You give us decision when you get
back. Sound fair?" Mary sounded.

"Thanks. I will know by then," Vicki stressed.

And so at the end of the week, Vicki packed a
small suitcase, and said goodbye to the other dogs
on premise. They were going to be fed and watered
and taken outside every day by one of the workers
at the market around the corner where she always
shopped. She went to pick-up her oldest dog after
work to take with her, and then Vicki went on her
merry way, down to the Tampa Bay area.

The couple stayed at a different hotel this time that
again allowed dogs and had a kitchen. Vicki told Ben

that she had paid for a week already. That meant to her that she could leave whenever she wanted during that week to begin her new life with the Texas corporation, or not. It happened to be, *or not.*

When they were buying food at the grocery up the street from the hotel in Clearwater, Vicki picked up a daily rag to look for jobs in the area. That afternoon she found a blurb that interested her. It read:

School is looking for a Spanish teacher, that was all, no school name, only a phone number to call.

Vicki called, and she was given an appointment time, with directions on how to get there.

The secretary had answered the school phone with, "Good afternoon, Shoreline Academy."

So Vicki did some research on the school and found it to be one of the most prestigious academies in Tampa Bay.

When she arrived at the school office, she found it loaded with administration. Each department head took part in the interview, asking her all types of tough academic questions. They recorded her responses. At the end, the head master told Vicki to expect a call next week, and he would tell her one way or another what their verdict was. He told her that they have interviewed about one hundred eighty applicants, and they have more interviews scheduled.

"That's fine," was all that Vicki could say, knowing that it would be extremely difficult and not in her plans to have to stay there another week, in order to wait for the administration's answer.

Feeling unhappy, but very hungry, because she had had no breakfast and only a bite to eat the night before, Vicki got into her car to look for a place to eat. She found a chain restaurant that was familiar to her, as she ate there all the time in northern Mississippi.

She wanted to eat a quick snack and go back to the hotel for a nap. She was very tired, to say the least. A homely man sat next to her. They talked for a bit, and he handed her his card.

"Call me if you want to go out for a fine dinner tonight on the water," he tempted her with his fine offer and the sound of his resonant voice.

Victoria awakened with the sound of the incessant ring of her cell phone. She did not know the number, so she hesitantly answered it. It was the academy.

"Victoria, this is Mrs. Jennings, the head master's assistant, and I am calling to offer you the Spanish teaching job for next school year. Congratulations."

"That is great. I thought you wouldn't know until next week," Vicki added.

"We did too, but after speaking with you, we made up our minds, and chose you for the position. You impressed everyone with your answers to their questions."

"Yes, yes, I will take the offer. Thank you," she said

"Great. Can you come by tomorrow morning to sign the contract?" the assistant asked her.

"Yes, of course I can," Vicki replied.

Victoria told Ben the good news when he got to the hotel that night, and he responded without any expression, "Good."

Vicki signed the contract over coffee. She had one month to move down there. She had so much to day, like fixing up the house for a sale, and finding a good realtor to sell, or even rent it. She knew this was the best thing for her, a new start in Florida.

The evening before, Vicki found a two bedroom loft down the street from the academy. The owner said he would allow dogs, and the rent was good. Vicki wrote a small deposit check for the six month lease and was given the keys.

Vicki couldn't contain her excitement that morning when she checked out of the hotel, giving the keys to Ben, before giving him a hug and a kiss.

"I love you. I'll call you when I get home. I have so much to do, like first sign a contract. I'm going to the school before I'm late," she shouted out to her Piranha.

"Love you, too. I'll take good care of the apartment. Talk later," and he turned to get on the elevator for the room, without kissing her, or even turning around to look her way as she left.

On the interstate the next morning, her court-report suitor called to invite her over to his home for lunch that he was preparing for the two of them. Vicki told him she was still driving on the interstate in Alabama and wouldn't be in town until that evening.

"That's fine. I'll wait," he assured her.

As soon as their call ended, another ring sounded, and it was her other *beau*, the former teacher. He invited Vicki to accompany his young son and him that same night to Beale Street. Vicki said that she would meet them there in the parking lot at eight.

She now anticipated these two dates, scheduled for the same evening and night.

"Can I make it work?" she grinned and asked herself, as she sped down the highway.

TWENTY-SIX

THE ACADEMY

Vicki stopped by her court reporter's mansion, knocked on the side door, and was escorted into a large, gourmet kitchen, with three ovens, six burners, and a grill. Vicki said that she could only stay for a few minutes, as she had a commitment that had just come up downtown. He continued cutting the vegetables.

Appearing hurt, he said, "I was preparing you one of my special concoctions. I also bought a very special vintage bottle of Pinot Noir. It goes perfect with this Italian dinner."

Not caring about his emotional stance, she assured him that she was sorry, but she had to go.

"Can we make it another time?" she asked him shyly.

"Yes, we can, but you've made a happy man very sad," he added slyly.

She continued to her home, changed her clothes and fed the dogs, and continued to Beale Street. There she met up with her former teaching associate and his eight-year old son. They went to dinner, which continued with dancing, until he started throwing back shots at the bar. He became quite intoxicated, as what he was best known for, and in his drunken state, she offered his son and him abode at her home for the night. He did not accept, said he was fine, and unbelievably made it back to his home near Nashville.

Vicki found a real estate agent the next morning who worked for a leading firm.

She signed a three-month contract, renewable after that, and set a price. She called Ben to tell him about the sale of the home, but there was no answer on the other end.

All was done, except for packing and moving. She would leave the furniture intact, so that she could sell the house, move the essentials now and come back for the rest after the sale. But she needed help, she thought. She called Ben's mother, the reborn Christian to ask for her help.

"We can load as much as you want in my truck. It holds a lot. When do you want to pack up and leave?" Peg asked.

"I have to be at work in three weeks, so sometime next week, maybe Tuesday," Vicki responded in a matter of fact way.

"Will do, sweetie. I will be her at seven in the morning to strap everything down, and we'll be off," Peg said.

"Thanks for helping us out. I really do appreciate it," Vicki responded.

The drive down to St. Pete was uneventful, sunny, not much traffic. When they arrived at their rental, Ben came flying out of the front door, hugging Vicki until she gasped her air. His mother just smiled and brought in the necessities from the back of the truck.

Vicki settled into her apartment life, with four dogs, sleeping only on a mattress on the floor. It reminded her of the old days, when they were building the house. Her life seemed routine, but predictable, which she loved. One night, however, while on a rampage, Ben let the air out of the tires of her car.

"Why did you do this? Now I can't get to work," she yelled.

"Because you haven't done anything for me lately, no money, no drugs no nothing," he answered her.

Crying, she called the school to tell them of the incident. She spoke to the head master who patched the call to security. The security guard, a former police officer, asked her to come and talk with him, and to take a cab in that morning.

"The school will pay for it. Just come and see me, please," he requested.

"I will," Vicki verified in short.

"You should really be careful, Vicki," the security guard stated. "That is not normal behavior. If a man gets mad, he just gets mad and blows it off. A man would never take air out of his own wife's tires, for any reason. What's his problem?"

"He has a bit of laziness, and mixed with his use of marijuana, it makes him mean. I don't know much about his condition, but I know that he is a bit of a manic depressive, and he won't see a doctor," Vicki gave him her full diagnosis of Ben.

"Well, I don't want to hold you up for class. I know you have a lot of work to do, but please be careful. You can always notify me if anything arises, okay?" he told her.

"Nothing will, but thank you," Vicki answered. She stayed at another female teacher's house that night.

Two days later, while walking from breakfast, Ben drove in the school yard, with a scowl on his elongated face. He stopped his truck suddenly, right in front of his wife.

"Where were you last night, you whore?" he screamed across the campus, for everyone to hear.

Vicki kept on walking towards her class.

"Answer me," her husband interjected.

"Leave me alone. I never want to see you again," she screamed out.

"Fine with me you slut, you whore," he lambasted her, as he screeched out of the parking lot.

Vicki told her teaching assistant, who told the security guard. She was invited once again into his office to talk about her marital situation.

"You need to leave him now. We will give you an apartment, near your class. It has a microwave and a sink, plus you can eat at the campus cafeteria all meals at no cost. You have to do this for your own safety, and the safety of others."

Vicki stayed in the one-room apartment on the school grounds for one month. When she went on the town late at night, she met weird, single men, like the butcher who wanted to pair her up with every woman who he saw, and the man who expounded on his business of ticket scalping at very high prices. She decided to just stay home and cry, watching psychological thriller movies on DVD. She had to pair this off with a bottle of red wine, however, to make each evening complete. She was bored out of her mind and felt like she did not have one reason to live.

Vicki remembered how her husband had stood by her side when she took her case up to Nashville, as they were driving down to Tampa for their cruise. She wanted to stop by the capital and give the governor her written memoirs of what transpired in the last school she was placed in. Vicki wrote everything, from the start, with the stabbing and bullying, up to the last, when the principal labeled Vicki a non-rehire for no reason at all, just because the school board had the power to do that. They seemed able to do this whenever they wanted and for whatever purposes.

She left her fifteen page report with the governor's secretary, as Vicki saw the governor being interviewed by the press at that very moment. She put the paper pile on her desk, and the secretary said that she would be sure the governor read it by the end of the day.

At the end of that month, Vicki turned on the television while making dinner, and was astonished by the top local news story of the day.....*All principals must be reviewed every year and must now sign annual contracts, regardless of tenure.*

"At least I helped change the system a little. At least now, no one has a *free pass.* They must account for their actions," she stated proudly to herself.

Vicki really did not like living in that small apartment. She missed having a husband, but hated the way she was treated by him most times. She heard that a former boyfriend of hers was now living in St. Petersburg, so she looked up his number on the internet, found it and called him.

David invited her over to his duplex for a "fun time", as he stated.

Once there, her ex-boyfriend drew out white lines of cocaine for the two to partake in.

"I don't do drugs, and I never have done them. You know that, so why'd you ask me here?" she questioned his ways.

"People can change and always do," he rectified himself. "I just thought you might like to have some fun, you know, with all the stuff you've been going through."

"No really. I need to go, have school tomorrow," she spoke.

"Alright. Hope I didn't upset you. You know you can call me anytime," he acknowledged.

"Yep," she said, as he walked her to her car.

When she got back to her apartment, she couldn't open the door with the key. The dead bolt was on. Then she realized that the dogs, who jump up at the door, at all hours of the day, must have inadvertently pushed the dead bolt and locked it. They were quite intelligent dogs too, and they were very mad that Vicki had stayed out for so long that night.

She called David on her cell and told him what happened. He came to rescue her. He tried a high window on the front of the apartment to see if it were unlocked, and it was. He then lifted her up to open it and put her through the unlocked window.

"I owe you one, David," she told him, rather shyly.

"I would have done this for anyone, Vicki. That's just in my nature. Do you remember all of the stupid stuff I used to do to help people? I got used and abused, but never changed, and never will," and he firmly held her hand in his and kissed her softly.

They wound up in her sofa-bed and had a night of ecstasy, one which she had not had for a long time. She felt like she needed it and was glad it happened.

TWENTY-SEVEN

THE APARTMENT

Vicki had a meager existence, living in a one-room old campus apartment, without a full kitchen to cook, which she wanted to do so desperately. She dreamed of having a fully-equipped kitchen again, one with a range, conventional oven, and dishwasher. She was tired of scrubbing each and every dish and pot by hand.

Since she moved in, she had been cooking every meal on a portable range she bought at the dollar store. It served its purpose well for Vicki. Most times, at the end of the school day, she was ready for peace and quiet. Grading homework should be done in the afternoon, not at night, she believed. And so, she hardly went to the cafeteria for dinner, but instead, remained in the slight comfort of her current abode. At least, she had the dogs there, and therefore, felt comfortable.

It was a good set up, walking next door to her class in the morning to work, and back again in the late afternoon to relax.

One night, to her surprise, her husband knocked on her door. She stared at him and said nothing, only felt hatred and betrayal.

"Can I come in? I need a place to stay. I've been sleeping in my truck for two nights now, and I'm cold. November in Florida can be chilly," he smiled cunningly.

"You are not allowed to step foot on this campus. If someone sees you here, they may call the police," she advised. "You better go now."

"Well, I can't. I have no place to go. I have been living in hotels and with Doug, since we left our apartment early. I'm glad the landlord didn't give us any grief for that move, you know?" Ben glared at Vicki.

Vicki walked out of the room.

"Don't leave when I'm talking to you," he grabbed her shoulder.

"Let me go. I have to get up early. I work," she said in a demoralizing tone.

"Can I sleep in this chair here at least?" he asked Vicki.

"Sure," she said. "Have at it. You must see a doctor about your mood swings, and if you don't, then I'm afraid we have to call it quits. I have already seen a divorce attorney, you know. He's just waiting on me to say yay or nay."

"Hey babe, let's go out looking for a house to rent, or even to buy. You know, like we used to?" he asked her anxiously, changing the subject.

"You didn't answer my question Ben. What's your answer?"

"I am doing well with my mood swings. I saw a friend of Doug's, who is in med school, and she says that is just anxiety on my part. Yes, only anxiety. Nothing's the matter with me," he confidently uttered, pulling out a joint from his tattered jean pocket.

"You can sleep in the bed, just stay on your side," Vicki caved into him. "You have to leave before dawn."

The rigorous routine of leaving before sunrise every morning and returning after dark was getting boring to Ben. The following Saturday morning, he took his wife out for breakfast at a cheap, but renowned local spot. Afterward, the couple left to go and scope the real estate listing they were interested in. The first one was a very average-looking, one-story, small, wood house, located in the most inconvenient part of St. Petersburg.

They looked at each other, upon leaving the property and said, "No."

The second parcel caught there eye, being a three story home, with two fireplaces and wood floors, and a nice, big kitchen. It had a warm feeling about it. The only problem was that while the house was located at the edge of the beautiful historic district of the city, it was also a stone's throw away from the highest crime zone of the city. It had a lot of room, however, coupled with a low monthly rent, and so they rented it.

She notified the academy of her desire to vacate and hired a cleaning crew to rid the small apartment of the excess hair, which was everywhere. It was hard to keep it spotless, being so small, and with countless dog hairs floating in the air.

Now having four large dogs that patrolled the new rental, they felt safe, pretty safe.

At times, Vicki stayed there alone into the night, when she wasn't working her second job. She took this job to help pay for the mortgage for the house in Mississippi. It was too hard for Vicki to pay for two places, on a teacher's salary, and Ben was still not much help.

Occasionally, he paid a utility or phone bill, but he always bought groceries for the two of them, nothing extravagant or gourmet, but at least it was food, she would always tell people.

They received a call on Vicki's cell the next weekend. It was the realty firm in Collierville. They announced that they have a buyer for the house.

"If you like their offer, you have a buyer. They already are qualified for a small loan. They would be paying three-quarters by cash. I will send you the contract express mail, and if you accept the offer, please sign it and date it, and send it back express. After that, I would set a date and time for the sale and the turnover of keys. You are able to come up here at a moments notice?" the wife of the real estate duo asked.

"We can always come up for a weekend, or a long weekend. I could take one day off and leave Thursday afternoon, so that we could sign on Friday, a business day," Vicki noted.

"We can work out all the details as soon as you accept the terms," she said. "Let me know as soon as possible."

When the offer and terms were placed on her door step the next afternoon, Vicki agreed on everything.

She phoned the husband of the duo and told him that the price was a little low, but still acceptable, but she couldn't replace the refrigerator with a brand-new larger one, which the buyer had requested.

"Can we just take it off the price offered? That would be simpler for me," Vicki interjected.

"I am sure that will be no problem. Probably better. They get to choose it," the agent affirmed. "I will be in touch, as soon as I know the date and time. Oh, and will you be bringing a lawyer?"

"I think I will," she said, remembering the lawyer who she used for her first home purchase.

Vicki was notified by email regarding the home sale a week later and provided with a date and time, as well as the title company that the buyers would be using. It was sad to be selling the house, she thought, but necessary. It had bittersweet memories.

They drove up using back roads this time. They both wanted to change up their driving routine, and the two routes up on seventy-five through Georgia, and across the pan handle on ten were definitely becoming routine.

She took off at lunch that Thursday. After lunch, she had only a planning period and two classes. She left classwork and homework with the principal, which she in turn, distributed to Vicki's students for their missed work on those two days. They left from their rental at about twelve thirty, making it up to Memphis in seventeen hours, a little longer because of the speed limits on the back roads.

Their closing was scheduled for two in the afternoon, so they slept at their Mississippi house for about six hours that morning. That worked out well for them.

They spent two nights there, leaving on Sunday morning with their remaining goods and furniture tied down to the back of the pick-up. It was quite an old-fashioned type of move, the type that pioneers used to do.

Taking the interstate now, they managed to get to their new home in record time.

They moved in their furniture and belongings to their rental, only to have it burglarized the next day, when the dogs were still at the kennel. Nothing was damaged or stolen, however, just rummaged through. They were looking for something of value, which was not found in the house. They took the air-conditioning unit from outside the window on the first floor. The couple didn't care, because it was winter, and it was cold.

Ben called the landlord. The landlord knew exactly who it was and was able to press charges against the individual. The individual happened to be the next door neighbor who had qualified for FHA loans, so had a bought a number of properties to rent out.

"I guess one of his air-conditioners broke, huh?" Ben jokingly asked the landlord.

The next day, the landlord called the two to offer them a much more appealing property, at a much more appealing address. They fell for the offer. The home overlooked the giant park and the canal and was very close to Tampa Bay. It was situated on a rolling green hill. This area was where ancient Indian mounds were located. The myth is that if they are tampered with in any way, bad events will occur.

"I don't know how anything worse could happen, than what's already happened," she informed Ben, as they read one of the historic plaques in the park.

Vicki ended up putting a deposit on the home, so that they could purchase it.

And with that twenty-five hundred dollar deposit, no one could put a claim on the property. It was stated in the contract. This amount that she laid out was from the sale of the home, but it still hit her hard. She used the money to pay off current billing statements, and she gave Ben a semester's worth tuition to a plumbing school in the area. She also bought herself a new sports car, a little luxury, but not a lot.

TWENTY-EIGHT

Rosser Park

And so they began a new life in the prestigious, historic, yet still somewhat seedy district of Rosser Park near downtown St. Pete. Vicki thought it beautiful and to look somewhat like the "Squirrel Hill" area of Pittsburgh, with all of its Indian mounds, disguised as hills.

Vicki loved living downtown, being able to ride a bicycle to the store every day to pick up groceries, and walking a few blocks to the bay was even better. At every special occasion when they had a fire work display, she could sit on her front porch and watch the display, no charge. It was heaven to her.

Ben opened a plumbing company of his own and was doing quite well. He had contracts at all of the hotels in St. Pete Beach. He was out a lot at night, on emergency calls. She knew that it was for real, because she heard the frantic conversations on the other line. Ben never wanted to leave at night, besides. Not when he was in dreamy, sleep land.

Vicki went with him every day after school and on the weekends to visit the different hotels of St. Pete Beach, as a means of promotion. It was fun for her. She thought it to be her calling.

Once the routine started creeping up on Ben, with the endless emergency phone calls at night, now all over the Tampa Bay area, he shut down and started smoking weed every chance he got. The stress was getting to him, as it always had.

One day, when coming home from school, Vicki saw a fire truck in front of her house. Peering off to the left, she saw one of her dogs being pulled up out of the canal water in front of their house.

The firemen told Vicki that the landlord had let the dogs out of the house when he went inside to inspect the refrigerator that was not working, as Vicki reported to him. When he opened the door, the four dogs came running out. Three returned right away.

The other, Monte, had jumped into the narrow canal in front and started swimming. A neighbor called the fire department and reported this. They swiftly came and retrieved "Monte" from the water.

This brought back bad memories of the time last year when Ben was angry, with no drugs in his system. Vicki was petting the female dog and loving on her in the apartment at the academy.

Ben asked, "So, she's more important than me? You don't have any money to give me, so out the dog goes," and he opened the apartment door and let her out.

The dog proceeded to swim in the canal, towards to the Gulf of Mexico. Vicki screamed and ran, following her dog down the canal and across the main street that the canal ran under.

Cars stopped, trying to help get her dog, but none could. Finally, an SUV stopped in the middle of the street. The driver took off the canoe that was strapped on top and rowed his way to her dog. He picked the dog up and put her in the canoe and proceeded to row his way back to where Vicki was standing, nervously waiting.

She cried so many "happy" tears and vowed never to speak to her husband again.

Of course, this never happened. It never did. Ben had some kind of a mesmerizing effect on his gullible wife. She had that quality about her and wished she could put an end to this part of her being, but she didn't know how to do it. Even though she was intelligent and had a high IQ, she wasn't "street-smart" with guys, especially good-looking ones like Ben.

Vicki remembered a beau she had and whom she met years before in Memphis, when she worked front desk at a luxury hotel. There she met a sexy man who she thought looked just like Brad Pitt. They had had a romance in Memphis, as well as in "The City of Angels", for several months, when she was separated from her ex-husband for one entire summer. Many times during their steamy affair he had called her gullible and said that she really needed to change that.

"It's really not that appealing my sweet, being so stupid," he patronized her one evening. She broke up with him the next day. The break-up only lasted for three days.

When Vicki eventually met Ben, not too long after her divorce, she thought that he was the most handsome man she had ever seen. She told him on many occasions that he was a cross between a couple of actors from the old screen, Cary Grant and Robert Taylor, whom she both adored. He would just shrug.

Vicki had a mental problem of her own. She was so in love with this mental abuser and thief that she always let him win. Being the loser in the game never bothered her, because she still had Ben.

"When I am without Ben in my life, I feel like I've lost everything," Vicki confided in a phone call to a friend from elementary school on one of their "break-up" nights.

"Well, you have to do what you have to do," her girlfriend hesitantly muttered.

Vicki's friends were true blue and never wanted to humiliate her. They wanted to tell her how they felt about her marriage with a "dictator", as her best friend called him one night in a rage. She stopped, however, before her opinionated behavior got too out of control. No one wanted to upset Vicki. Everyone seemed to love and respect her, even acquaintances and co-workers. Everyone that is, except for her husband, Ben.

TWENTY-NINE

THE NEW HOUSE

After the hurricane that threatened them, so much so that they left, with dogs, in Vicki's car. They made it to Orlando, where Ben's mother had made hotel reservations for them, and the dogs.

His mother knew of Vicki's financial stress, so she did this for them. His aunt also knew of Vicki's distress, liked her so much and felt sorry for her being with her nephew.

His aunt, Cathy, or Cat, as she was better known by, was two years younger than Vicki, was a nice lady, but had a big drug problem and anger management issues toward her immediate family. Vicki thought that mental problems and addictions must run through their family.

Cat had been the one to whom Ben sold her jewelry. Cat had her problems, but at least she was true and honest.

She came over to the house, as the concrete truck was pouring a small patio in the back yard, so the house would be more sellable. Vicki could pay this very small business only with an expensive dining room table and chairs. The two brothers were happy to receive this, as they shared a house together with not many furnishings, as they told Vicki.

Cat reached into her pocket and pulled out the ring that Ben had stolen from her jewelry box, when on a rampage for drugs.

Vicki gasped and ran over to hug her.

Cat told her, "I had to bring this over to you. There is no way I would ever sell your personal stuff. I cannot believe he gave this to me to sell for him. I gave him the money he wanted, or my mother did. She told me not to sell your stuff either. He's despicable. I'm so sorry honey, but if I were you, I would divorce him right away."

"He'll change. I know he will," Vicki stressed.

"Whatever. I'll be praying for you," said Cat, as she left the house.

Her prayers must have finally worked, because on her home from work one day, she saw a small house and called the real estate agent to get more details. She found the price offered to be stimulating, and the inside mortgage company's rates to be even more appealing.

Vicki set up a day and time when she could view the small property, located between a lush neighborhood and a poor one. These type of median neighborhoods run rampant through the city, she thought.

This desire of wanting to buy her own place was because of the precedent of what happened that morning. Vicki was to go to an all-day teacher's meeting. It was a hot day in late April, so she didn't want to wear sleeves of any type. So, she slipped on a sleeveless black silk top and black jeans.

When Ben took sight of his wife, he flew into a stout rage, throwing objects around the room, like the feminine sex does on occasion, not the male.

"Don't you ever wear that slut outfit out," he reprimanded Vicki. "Now go change into something more ladylike."

"But everyone is casual today. Some are even wearing shorts and tank tops, they told me," Vicki defended herself.

"I don't care. They are all sluts. You should see the way they look at me, and have talked to me. Don't ever be like them," he commanded her.

So, she did as he commanded, but only for one last time. In her eyes, that was the last straw, the **real last straw**. All of the other straws had blown away in the wind, when he put on his seminal act of kindness. This straw, however, she was holding onto, never letting it go. She had made her decision, and she was ready. She would buy the house, leave Ben, and finally divorce him.

Victoria put in her bid for the house the following morning. She offered three thousand dollars less than what the house was reduced to. She got a call back, when she was fixing their famous spaghetti and pineapple. The agent informed Vicki that the sellers had taken her price, and the closing would probably be set for late next week. He would call her about that tomorrow.

Relieved, she sighed and told him to call her back in the morning, not in the evening.

"Sure thing, Victoria," Massey acknowledged.

Massey was an elderly gentleman who had been a chemical engineer and was now embarking on a career as a real estate agent in his retirement years. This was the second house he had sold, and he was ecstatic. So was Vicki. She did not show her enthusiasm to her now husband, but he knew something was up.

"Who was that?" Ben asked Vicki, as she was simmering the sauce.

"The headmaster, about a student," she lied to him.

"I don't think so. It was some guy talking about 'a sale'."

"I don't know what you're saying. You're mistaken. Please honey, not now. I'm so tired, but I still managed to fix your favorite for you," and he looked down in the skillet smelled the sauce, and smiled with scintillation. She had him, for once in her life.

THIRTY

THE RESTRAINING ORDER

Vicki packed her bags in the middle of the night and left her pieces of furniture behind, not that she had many. She put her bags in the trunk of her car and went back upstairs to sleep with her husband for one more night.

The next morning, she awoke with a start. Ben was still asleep. Finally, he woke up and climbed out of bed, starving. Vicki said they were out of everything.

"Let's go to *Margo's* for some eggs and coffee," suggested Ben.

"Okay. Let's go," Vicki responded, wanting to get this over with, then leave, for good.

When the two got back, with such stuffed bellies that they could barely walk, Ben fell back to sleep. Vicki left the rental house, and never came back. She traveled one hundred avenues to the East, to the office where the signing was to take place.

After she signed, giving no money for a down payment, she was handed a set of keys. She then traveled to her new home, excited, but still not knowing what to expect from recent events.

All night, her cell was ringing, keeping her up late on a Saturday night. She turned on a movie channel, where she watched horror films of bygone days. The ringing finally stopped.

The next morning the ringing began again, and it never stopped all day. She never answered.

At school the next day, she changed her mailing address with the accounting office so that they could mail her check each week to the right place, especially over the summer. This was where she went wrong, but she had no other choice. Ben retrieved Vicki's address through a girl in accounting who was a friend of one of the elementary teachers with whom she taught, and with whom he flirted, and with whom he probably had intimate times.

That night he showed up at her front door, knocking violently.

Vicki never answered it.

Ben left, then showed up again at two in the morning, almost beating the door down.

Again, she did not answer the door, but instead called the police. They sent a patrol car to her residence, but by then, Ben was gone.

The police car was still out front of her house the following morning. Before she left for school, the police officer out front motioned for Vicki to come over to talk to him, and which she did.

"You really do need to take out a restraining order on that guy down at the station. That way, if he comes near you, or your residence, you can have him arrested," he suggested to the damsel in distress.

"I probably should, because he might come back again," Vicki said.

"You can count on it," he said with certainty, and he drove off toward the sunrise.

"I will then," she acknowledged and started the process.

The couple had been trying to get pregnant since the day they married but with no luck, and it had been almost five years.

At Vicki's next gynecologist visit, which happened to be at the very end of April, she asked the doctor if he could perform extensive tests on her to see what the matter was. She told his office that she now had insurance through the school to pay for these tests. Vicki knew these fertility tests would be expensive, but at last she would be able to finally see if she could ever have babies.

The tests came back forty-eight hours later, and the doctor called Vicki into his office for a conference. Ben's calls stopped. Vicki wondered why, but was pleased. She now felt safe and sane. He had been driving her crazy, like everything was her fault. Ben had always made her feel this way.

Ben had believed that Vicki was made of money. She was just keeping it a secret, not even letting anyone know. He didn't want to have anything more to do with his wife, now that he knew for sure from his lawyer, who his mother had hired to represent him in a divorce, that she did not have a cent to her name, and really never had. She had not lied to him.

"I can't believe I stayed with that old hag for so long. She had nothing. No, nothing like you have, babe, and you don't even need to have one dollar," he slyly said to his new landlord. She was eight years older than Ben, and loaded with cash.

People all around the city said that they saw that woman spending lavishly on Ben, day and night.

Vicki saw commercials advertising Ben's plumbing company, that she was sure were financed through his landlord. No, Ben did not need Vicki any longer.

And Vicki, for sure, did not need Ben any longer. She met with her gynecologist that morning and found out the truth. All along, Ben had told Vicki that he had a high sperm count, as was provided by his doctor in Memphis. This was false, another one of his incessant lies. Ben was the one who was infertile, not Vicki.

Her doctor advised her that she was completely normal, fertile and healthy and able to start having children right away. Vicki was pleased. Ben had taken too much out of her being, and she wasn't going to let him do it anymore.

The next morning at sunrise, she got up to go to the school. Upon entering her classroom, she was served with divorce papers from her husband.

"This is such a game he's playing. Geez, let it be," she moaned. "Well, he got the divorce going first, so he thinks he won."

A letter came in the mail the following week requesting a mediation that was requested by Ben, the petitioner. Vicki went to the meeting and waited, along with members of counsel, and waited, and waited. Ben never came. The lawsuit was thrown-out.

Vicki, thereafter, met with a divorce lawyer in Tampa who proceeded to have her husband served with papers the next morning, at his landlord's home. Her address was not private. Everyone in the city knew this woman, and where she resided. Ben was fuming mad.

He got in his car and headed to his wife's residence. While there, pounding at her door, she called the police and told them that her husband was at her door and shouldn't be.

"I recently took out a restraining order on him. I was advised to do so. He can't be at my front door, and he is," she frantically told the nine-one-one operator. The police car must have been patrolling the neighborhood, because it arrived at her house in less than two minutes. He tried to run, but was apprehended and taken to the county lock-up.

Ben stayed in the county jail for two months, awaiting trial. He was not able to provide bail. His mother was in town, but she couldn't provide it for him either, because her property was out of state, so no bail company would loan her the money on that property.

Vicki kept up with Ben's stay in prison by looking it up on the internet every week. School was now out, so she had some extra time to secure her property and keep a close eye on who was around her at all times, and where Benjamin was at all times.

During his first week of incarceration, Ben was served with divorce papers. Their divorce date was to be determined. He screamed and cried all night in the lock-up.

"How could she do this to me? My life is ruined," he declared to whomever was listening.

Ben never saw or heard hide nor hair from his landlord girlfriend. Vicki found this out from visitor lists at the jail that her attorney viewed. He was not permitted to make calls during his temporary stay at the facility.

And so the pendulum swings..., she smiled and thought to herself in smugness.

THIRTY-ONE

The Divorce

As soon as Ben was released from the county jail, a court hearing was set.

It was scheduled to be held in one of the judge's chambers. It was supposed to be short and sweet, but became long and vicious, until the ending moment of sweetness.

Ben was not dressed properly, for a court hearing, and was thirty minutes late and had sweat on his brow from running to meet his appointment. At the table, the judge asked if it were to be a straight forward split, with no attributes on either side.

Vicki said, "Yes."

Ben said, "No. I need more."

Vicki replied, "I have nothing."

"You got something from the sale of the house. I need some of that. I built your house for you. I tore up carpet and installed wood flooring in the living room of the new house. I was your husband, Vicki. I need some money," Ben blurted out.

The table was now filled with yawners who quickly exited the room.

The judge suggested that the two straighten out the proceeds amongst themselves.

The soon-to-be divorcees decided on an amount of five thousand dollars to be distributed from the proceeds of the house sale to Ben. Ben's name was not even on the deed, so everyone felt like that was more than fair. That would leave Vicki with a ten thousand earning, which wasn't too bad for only living there for one year. They hadn't had the time or money for fix-ups either.

Ben looked happy now and was set for a little while. Vicki knew this money wouldn't last him long. He went through it like water.

Ben and Vicki hugged, and they cried when the divorce was granted, but Vicki went off with her new-beloved, thereafter, the one who rescued her at the truck stop in Central Florida, and the one who concernedly went with her to the courtroom for the hearing that day.

THIRTY-TWO

KARMA

Vicki and her new love, Joe, spent nine long, grueling, but loving years together before they tied the knot. Vicki and Joe have now been married for twenty-five, blissful years, and they have four beautiful children, three sons and one daughter. Vicki wouldn't trade her world for anything, and if she had to pay her dues to achieve a life like the one she was now living, she would do it all over again.

Vicki and Joe had a five acre ranch south of Tampa Bay, where they raised their kids and parked Joe's "outlaw" Peterbilt. Later, the couple retired in the Keys.

Once married, Vicki landed a job with a home decorating company in Bradenton. Joe had a small trucking company, where he and two other drivers hit the highway each and every week, delivering produce to the forty-eight states.

One of their sons became valedictorian and received a full scholarship to the Air Force Academy in Colorado Springs. Another went to Dartmouth to pursue law, and the other son became a trucker, like his hero father. Their daughter became a teacher, like her heroin mother.

Vicki almost forgot that she was ever married to Ben, or for that matter, that he even existed. She was free, happy....like her old self again. She thought of when her best friend was moving down from Memphis to be closer to her. Vicki flew up, helped Kerry pack her belongings in boxes to load into the twenty-six foot moving van that Vicki was to drive the next day, after two unskilled movers packed Kerry's furniture and boxes without weight being distributed evenly. Vicki felt the truck shake and shimmy a bit while traveling through Mississippi. She managed to grab hold of the wheel and right the load, during the two instances that it occurred. Kerry never felt it. She was asleep.

Once in Florida, Vicki glanced at her watch and realized that she would be late to the criminal court hearing, for which she was subpoenaed to testify. Noticing that she had very little fuel left, she quickly headed straight for the exit. Her friend went inside to pay for the fuel.

As she did, Vicki was hit in the back of the head with some type of shell, while her door was open, and she fell out, far from the truck, and onto the concrete. Blood gushed out of her head, turning her into a red head. Her best friend came out. Vicki was lying in a pool of blood, screaming. Tall, thin Kerry sprinted inside for help.

Out ran a nice-looking, well-built man who came to Vicki's rescue. He ended up becoming her prince charming. Prince Charming eventually asked Vicki to marry him, and so their blessed life proceeded.

It was obvious to all parties involved that Ben had something to do with the incident, as Vicki was scheduled to testify against him in one hour. The district attorney said the appointed judge, she felt, was ready to convict him for a long, long time for not abiding the restraining order on several occasions, with phone calls and his front door visit. Ben and his mother knew this, hence they took action.

They hired two thugs to follow the truck and keep Vicki from testifying, using whatever means possible.

After an hour at the hospital emergency room, the incident was declared as a non-life-threatening act. She was released and taken back to their moving van, along with her best friend, by one female police investigator who didn't believe her story and thought that she had staged the whole episode in order to sue the national truck-stop fuel and gasoline station. Vicki knew this and couldn't wait to be away from her grip.

Once at the truck, it was decided that Kerry should be the one to now drive the straight-job truck. A phone call to the county court was made to describe in depth what took place....a very justifiable reason for not showing up in court. Vicki's friend handled the truck well, that was, until the load started shifting even more, as if someone had tampered with the load making it much more uneven, while the truck had been sitting unattended.

Vicki's friend couldn't hold the truck upright any longer. The truck went down on its side and skidded for about one hundred yards until it stopped. Both parties were lifted up through the broken windshield, alive and fairly well...but dazed.

Life returned to normal for Vicki and Kerry.

Two days later, Vicki asked her best friend if she still had the phone number that the *guy at the fuel pump* gave to her after the incident.

In the kitchen trash can, Kerry found and looked in her beat-up, torn-up purse, but saw nothing, only tattered and frayed pieces of paper and leather. She did notice one small, white, sturdy paper at the bottom, however, and brought it up closer to her eyes. She gleamed. It displayed his name and phone number, the only thing inside her purse that remained intact and totally readable, turning this into a real Cinderella story.

Justice was not served, however. Ben's and his mother's plan eventually worked to their advantage.

At the new trial, a novice judge was assigned, who took mercy on Ben's pleas.

The judge gave him only probation.

The divorce was finally granted, as Vicki paid ransom money to Ben for the final time from the proceeds of her home in St. Petersburg.

It didn't matter to her though. **She was finally free**.

Cinderella was now off and running with her prince charming, awaiting her spectacular destiny with a man who vowed to take care of her in every way, and he did what he promised.

The glass slipper definitely fit her foot.

Oh, and Ben…well, Ben did run through his money like water and became a *beggar* in South Tampa.

And so the pendulum swings…

VICKI'S EPILOGUE

*T*hinking about it now, I should have never stayed by Ben's side. No, not after that kooky evening at dusk when he drove me to the cemetery in Collierville. He got such a thrill that it sent chills down my spine, as he walked inside the metal gates, around each grave with care. He even pulled up a chair and sat down.

Ben felt the most comfortable there, sitting in the middle of that graveyard. I should have known from that point on that he was damaged goods.

All I can say is you live and you learn, and you never repeat the bad. Am I right?

And so the pendulum swings...

The End